FROM WHERE I STAND

ff

FROM WHERE
I STAND

Susan Price

faber and faber
LONDON · BOSTON

First Published in 1984
by Faber and Faber Limited
3 Queen Square London WC1N 3AU
Reprinted 1986
Typeset by Set Fair Limited
Printed in Great Britain by
Thetford Press Limited, Thetford, Norfolk
All Rights Reserved

British Library Cataloguing in Publication Data

Price, Susan
From where I stand.
I. Title
823'914 [J]   PZ7

ISBN 0-571-13247-2

1

Everybody going to school.

Sharon Walker and Joanne Burton always walked to and from school together. They were in the same class for every subject, and lived near each other too, and had gone to the same Junior school. So they were friends.

Joanne was skinny and pretty, with long, wavy dark hair. She always looked smart in her school clothes, and Sharon sometimes envied her prettiness. Sharon was a little overweight; her face was chubby and she had a slight double chin, but she wasn't overweight enough for it to matter. No one teased her about it. There were other people who had been established as the school fatties back in Infant and Junior school, and they drew all that kind of teasing. Nobody bothered to look round and notice that other people had grown fat too. So most of the time Sharon didn't think of herself as fat. She saw herself as a sporty, slangy, tough girl — much tougher than Joanne who always came to school in a skirt. The school rules allowed girls to wear trousers, provided they were the school colour of navy blue, and Sharon wore trousers all the time, except when they hadn't been washed or dried in time by her mother.

There had been a programme on the television about the French Resistance, and in it there had been a girl named Natalie who had always worn trousers and a mannish

7

checked jacket, smoked cigarettes and carried a sub-machine gun on her hip. Sharon had watched that programme every week, just because of Natalie. Until the summer before her hair had been long, but after watching Natalie for a week or two, she had begun to beg her mother to allow her to have her hair cut short. Her mother, and her aunt, and her older cousin had all tried to dissuade her, because her hair was so lovely and a true blonde. They had said that long hair was coming back into fashion, and she'd be sorry when she was older if she had it cut. Sharon didn't try to explain that she wanted her hair like Natalie's — she had known that they would only scoff — but had stubbornly pleaded for permission to have it bobbed. Eventually her mother had found the money for her to have it cut and shaped at 'Chez Davina's'. With her hair cut short, wearing trousers, a blouse she could pretend was a shirt, a jacket, and a khaki bag slung over her shoulder, Sharon felt that she was close to Natalie's image. She was always looking for chances to get even closer. It made her happy when Joanne found something too heavy for her to move, or couldn't unwrap something, or couldn't unscrew the lid of a jar. Sharon loved to do it for her, and to tease Joanne about being weak. She loved to cross roads, dodging the cars, while Joanne was still timidly at the kerb; she loved to climb walls and fences that Joanne wouldn't climb because she was afraid of getting hurt, or spoiling her clothes. Then she felt exactly like Natalie: practical, capable and clever. Joanne would have been no good to the Resistance. She always wore such fussy shoes; she wouldn't have been able to run through the woodland, carrying a message. She wouldn't have thrown herself into the mud with a sub-machine gun. It would have dirtied her clothes.

"You done your history Shaz?" Joanne asked.

Sharon nodded.

"Can I copy yours at break, then?"

"You can — it's no good though. I rushed through it, so I

8

could go out." This was a lie — but, with Joanne, she kept up an image of someone who was always going out, to discos and parties. In fact, she had taken a book of her father's up to her bedroom and had spent all the evening reading it. The book was about the Norwegian Resistance during the Second World War. She would have preferred one about the French Resistance, but her father didn't have one, and she supposed that the Norwegian Resistance had been much the same as the French . . . It wasn't like the programme, though. Much of the book described hours and hours of watching ships and airfields through binoculars, and then radioing England with accounts of what had been seen, and weather forecasts. Weather forecasts! There had been, as yet, no blowing-up of trains, machine-gunning Germans, or rescuing airmen.

"Where d'you go?" Joanne asked.

"Oh — just around. Y'know," Sharon said. "Nowhere interesting."

"You're lucky getting to go out at all," Joanne said sulkily. They had reached the place where the road tipped up and ran down a steep hill. Their school, the Edward Brownheath School, was at the bottom.

Kamla Momen got off the bus outside the Green Man and stood at the kerb, waiting to cross. She was short, only five feet tall, and thin. Her trouser-suit was well brushed and pressed, the trousers sharply creased down the front, and with her shiny briefcase in one hand she looked far more self-assured than she ever actually felt.

Seeing the road clear, she pushed her spectacles up her nose, flicked back her long, heavy plaits with the white ribbons and, holding her head well up and swinging her case, crossed to the opposite side. She always made a point, when she felt she was on show, of walking proudly, as if she knew she was the best. She thought it the best disguise for fear. On the other side of the road, sitting on the garden wall of a house, were some boys, English boys, four of them. They watched her with stolid faces as she came towards them. She recognized that they were unfriendly, but she wouldn't change course to arrive on the pavement at a distance from them, or lower her head defensively. They were younger than she, and so owed her some respect, even if they were too ignorant to know it. She stepped on to the pavement directly in front of them, and gave them back a stare before starting down the hill to the school. While she was looking at them they didn't say anything, but as soon as she had gone a little way past, one of them said "Paki."

Kamla took another step, while the boys sniggered behind her, and the word, "Paki" was repeated. Her first impulse was to ignore it and go on; but then she thought, no, why should she ignore it, why should she accept it? That was what they counted on. She stopped, and turned, and looked at the boys. They rubbed their soles on the pavement, looked at each other and tittered. One stared at her aggressively, his pale blue eyes fixed wide, his broad, pink and white face trying to take on an expression of boldness. Kamla said, "Thank you very much. That's a nice compliment."

That confused them. They had insulted her, and she thanked them. The aggressive one said, "You're thick, you are."

Kamla smiled at that. "In Urdu," she explained, " 'paki' means 'pure'. So thank you." She turned again, gave her briefcase a big swing, and went on down the hill. She knew that they would be pulling childish faces behind her back, but she didn't care. She had stood up for herself, and she felt proud of that.

As she reached the school gates, a group of six Indian girls arrived from the other direction. She knew most of them, and had spoken to all of them at one time or another, but she wouldn't have described any of them as friends.

They were Hindu or Sikh. There were few Moslems at the Edward Brownheath School, and most of them were in the younger years. Most Moslem girls from her own area had gone to an all-girls' school nearby; but in the year Kamla had changed schools there hadn't been enough places, and so she had to take the long bus-ride to the Edward Brownheath. It was lonely, because the people she knew at school, she never saw at home; and her home friends were not with her at school. Nor did she find it easy to make friends. Looking at the ever-changing alliances between other people, especially the English girls, she thought that perhaps she took friendship too seriously. But she intended to go on doing so. It was not a bad thing to have learned to be self-reliant and content with her own company, especially since she planned to be a doctor, perhaps even a surgeon. People in those professions had to be prepared to look after themselves, make their own decisions, and find themselves in disagreement with others. Her parents were more concerned about her loneliness than she was. Every-time someone else had a brick thrown through their window, or petrol poured down their door, her mother spent several days fretting about her having to travel so far away from her family's protection. But both Kamla and her father thought it best for her to finish her secondary education at the school where she had begun it. After all, when she went to Medical School, she would have to move right away from home, and her mother would have to get used to it.

One of the Sikh girls, Parvinder, beckoned to her, and Kamla went over. In the year before, when Kamla had been in the fifth year and Parvinder in the fourth, they had often partnered each other in mixed form P.E. lessons. Parvinder began to talk to her in English, but the other girls, though turning to smile at Kamla, continued to talk in a language she couldn't understand. She could speak Bengali well, almost as fluently as she spoke English; and she knew a little Urdu and a little Arabic. She was rather sorry that English was her best language. When she was older, she thought, she would go back to Bangladesh and perfect her Bengali.

"I didn't want to come this morning," Parvinder said, putting her hand at the small of her back and frowning. "My period started last night, and I feel terrible. But my mother — oh!"

Kamla was a little shocked that Parvinder should talk so freely about such things, and said nothing. She felt some admiration, and considerable liking, for Parvinder, who, as soon as she was out of her mother's sight, let her long hair loose so that it hung all down her back and flew about in the wind, and opened her coat, and pulled her belt tight to show off her waist. She was always answering teachers back and being cheeky with them, in a way that made Kamla feel dull-witted and charmless

"Still, it only lasts three days now, my period," Parvinder said. "That's a good thing. Do you know how long it used to last?"

Kamla felt obliged to ask her how long.

"Two weeks! It was awful — I was going to kill myself, you know — I hated it. But it only lasts three days now, so that's all right — except that it hurts the first couple of days. Does it hurt you?"

Kamla grew a little hot as she nodded and said, "Mmm."

"I've got this terrible pain in my back," Parvinder said. "And in my belly. I feel rotten."

"Come to the Nurse and get some aspirin," Kamla said. She was a sixth former and could go into the school before the bell rang. As they hurried towards the teachers' and sixth formers' entrance, a blue mini passed them.

The mini was driven by Mags Firth, with Jenny Griffiths in the passenger seat. It was Jenny's first term of teaching. Her fair hair hung loose about her shoulders, and her face was completely made-up, with foundation, powder, eyeliner, mascara, blusher and lipstick. In her bag she had a make-up kit, to replace what was rubbed off. It had taken her twenty minutes that morning to apply it, but it was worth all the trouble because of the confidence it gave her. The last look in the mirror had told her that she was quite startlingly pretty. Without the make-up she thought that she looked awful — as plain as Mags. She looked sideways at Mags's rough and mottled cheek, and wondered how she could get through the day knowing that she looked like that. Without make-up Jenny knew that she would feel a mess, guilty and open to criticism. She wouldn't be able to concentrate on anything.

Mags Firth had one hand on the wheel, and one hand tapping on her knee as she hummed to herself. Her clothes were almost scruffy — jeans and a cable-knit sweater, with thick socks instead of nylons. She was thirty-four. Braking the mini outside the school, she looked across at Jenny, feeling agreeably older, stronger and wiser. She still enjoyed the novelty of thinking of a twenty-one-year-old as "just a kid."

"Listen," she said, "are you going down to the Annexe this morning?"

Flustered, Jenny opened the little bag on her knees and sorted through it for her timetable. She already knew it for that day, but she had to look at it again before she would commit herself. "Um — I don't think so — I — here it is — I'm there all afternoon, though."

Mags had been waiting patiently. "I can't give you a lift then. I'm only there this morning, after break. Have you got a lift for this afternoon?" Jenny shook her head. "Ask around when we go in. Somebody with a car will be going down there." Seeing Jenny's alarm, she added "No one will mind you asking. The running of this school depends on people giving lifts, believe me."

Jenny nodded, but everything about her expression and movements told Mags that she was determined not to draw attention to herself by asking for a lift. She would say nothing to anyone, and would struggle on and off a bus with all the books she needed for teaching at the Annexe, and she would be late because the buses were so unreliable; and that would be a black mark against her. Mags knew. She had, through shyness, done similar stupid things herself when she had been younger. "I know!" she said, bounding forward to pull open the doors of the staff entrance. "I'll introduce you to Les Stewart. I'm sure he's going there." She glanced at Jenny and saw that she was shrinking, but grateful. Mags felt a small stirring of contempt. How long are you going to go on expecting other people to look after you, girl? she thought.

Before going out to the car with her father, Cherie Reed ran up to her bedroom to check on her appearance. She put her face close to the mirror and then drew back and turned it from side to side, considering the overall effect. Were the foundation and powder smooth? Was the blusher too obvious? No, she looked wonderful. She knew that you weren't supposed to think well of yourself, but surely so long as she didn't tell anyone else, it was all right to admit that she *was* beautiful. She put her hands under her long red hair and lifted it to feel its weight, letting it go to admire the way it fell, in a wave, over her shoulders and down her back, almost to her knees. It took hours to dry when she washed it, but that was the price you had to pay to have such beautiful hair. She'd always been in trouble about it at school until she'd gone into the sixth form. The teachers had kept on at her to tie it back in a miserable pony-tail. Now she was in the sixth, they left her alone, and she wore it loose all the time. She had to carry a brush and comb with her, and she brushed it out when she got to school, at break, at lunch, and before she left at half-three. It got into terrible knots otherwise.

Her father shouted, and she pulled her skirt straight, and

smoothed her soft, fluffy blue sweater over her hips. Then she couldn't resist turning sideways to admire her figure from that angle, and putting her foot up on her vanity-table to look at her legs, and see how pretty her feet looked in her high-heeled shoes. And then she had to have yet another look at her eye make-up, just to be absolutely sure, and, while she was staring into the mirror, she smiled at herself in different ways: tenderly, mischievously, little girl-ishly. . . . "Cherie!" her father yelled from the bottom of the stairs. "If you don't come now, I'll go without you."

She knew that he wouldn't, but she hurried down the stairs. "You're too young to be in charge of a figure like that," her father said, and he tried to smack her bottom as she passed him. She twitched out of the way, feeling pleased and silly at the same time. Then he spoiled it by yelling, "Don't say you've got to fetch things now!" as she made for the living room. That wasn't fair. If he thought she was pretty, he shouldn't yell at her like that.

She grabbed her coat and bag from the settee, and her mother said, "Cherie, you shouldn't keep your father waiting. He's got to go to work."

"Me will only be a second, Mummy," Cherie said, and went out to her father, who was waiting with the door open.

"Come on, Killer," he said, and led the way to the car. He opened the door for her, and shut it after her, before going round to the driver's seat himself.

The school wasn't far. As they drove up to the main entrance, they passed a large group of Indian girls; and a black boy with two white girls strolled across in front of the car. Mr Reed said, "I bet you're browned-off, going to this school, aren't you?" He looked at her with the half-laughing face that he always used to signal a joke.

Cherie gave a little giggle, then bit her lip as if to stop herself laughing; then giggled again as if the joke had been so funny that she really couldn't help it. Her mock-disapproval pleased her father, who was laughing now, both at his own joke, and at its shocking her.

He turned serious as he drew the car up. "It's no laugh, though, is it? They come over here, have the best our education system can give — and I'm paying for it." Cherie released the catch on the door. "Give us a kiss before you go, darlin'."

Mr. Kendle, the Deputy Headmaster, was crossing the entrance hall when she went in. He glanced in her direction, and Cherie said, "Dood morning, Mr. Kenduw," using the soft voice and babyish lisp which she habitually affected. Mr. Kendle stopped and looked at her, and she smiled shyly.

"Well, good morning, Cherie," Mr. Kendle said, and his tone was unmistakably meant to convey admiration for her beauty, as was the look he gave her. "How are *you* today?"

"Oh, I'm vewy well, Mr. Kenduw — are oo, sir?"

"I am, Cherie, and all the better for your asking — but I'm in a hurry — excuse me." He continued across the entrance hall to his office, but he turned and gave her another smile as he went through the door. She went on her way, feeling elated. Such little things can make people happy, she thought, just a look or a smile. She could write a poem about that. She had written one or two poems, and one had been published in the school magazine.

Before, and between, lessons the sixth form assembled in the library. At the central table, where Cherie and her friends usually sat, she saw Kamla Momen standing and talking to Barbara Jones. A brief distaste passed through Cherie's mind. She thought it impudent of Kamla to stand there, out of her usual place — but then her friend, Jane, came up and she forgot all about Kamla for a while.

Kamla saw Cherie, saw her glance, and far more definite dislike rose in her mind. She had specific reasons for disliking Cherie: reasons that Cherie had probably forgotten all about. When Kamla had first started at the school, an isolated and frightened little first-year (doing her utmost to appear calm and self-confident) Cherie had led a campaign against her. Just two or three days after that first term had started, the class were left alone by the teacher, and the children had begun walking about, taking stock of their new companions. Many of them were with old friends from their primary school, but Kamla was entirely alone, and she sat alone, tense with suspicion and nervousness. If someone had offered to make friends, she would have been glad, but she wasn't sure how to begin herself. And Cherie had shouted out, "Hey, we've got a blackie!" and led a band of girls to her desk, to ask her insulting questions. Cherie hadn't had a lisp then. Kamla still winced inwardly when she remembered the incident. The girls had laughed and grown excited in the ugly way people do when they know they are being vicious but don't care, and are enjoying not caring.

Cherie had certainly changed her style a lot since then, but Kamla remembered that incident, and others like it, whenever she heard Cherie's sweet, breathy lisp.

2

Kamla's first lesson was Chemistry. There were only nine people in the class, seven boys and two girls, Kamla and Barbara Jones. They sat at one end of the front table, and the boys sat at the other. Barbara was a quiet girl too, and so the boys often made both of them the butt of sniggering jokes. If the teacher was in the storeroom, or marking, one of them would lean over and tell the girls some dirty joke, just to see if they would be embarrassed. Barbara usually smiled, and that was enough to satisfy them. They would crow childishly and say, "Oh, she's laughing, look — she gets it!" As if that was astonishing. Kamla always refused to smile. She didn't see why she should, just to please these boys.

They had been doing work on acids, and Mr. Lofts asked what would happen if they combined an acid with a substance opposite to it in composition. After a moment of silence, Kamla put up her hand. She saw the teacher look at her, and then past her to one of the boys. "Don't you know, Stephen?" he asked.

Stephen looked at the book in front of him and shook his head. "David?" Mr. Lofts asked. "How about you, Darren?"

How about *me* ? Kamla thought. *I* know the answer.

But Mr. Lofts ignored her, though her arm was still in

the air, and said, "Adam? No? Bob? Michael, then?"

This is a comedy, Kamla thought, lowering her arm, which was beginning to ache. He had seen her ready to answer, and had asked seven people who didn't know in preference to her. Finally the teacher turned towards the two girls, and she half-raised her arm again. The teacher said, "Barbara, how about you?"

Kamla's exasperation showed on her face as she lowered her arm once more. This was always happening, in every lesson, ever since she had started school. She was always the last to be asked, and the last to be visited when they were doing experiments, so she hardly ever got any help, or a chance to ask questions.

Barbara smiled and shook her head.

The teacher signed wearily and said, "Kamla, then."

He sounded so disgusted at having to ask her that Kamla was on the point of refusing to answer. But that would be to behave as stupidly as those sniggering boys. She said sourly, "You get a salt, and water."

"Right! Why does it always have to be Kamla who answers?"

Mr. Lofts began to write out on the board why the result of the experiment would be a salt and water, and Kamla's thoughts drifted away from Chemistry. Why were girls *always* asked last, she wondered, and Asian girls last of all?

For Sharon and Joanne, the first lesson was Home Economics. It began with their waiting in the corridor outside the Home Economics room. They were only second years, so they weren't allowed to go into classrooms without a teacher. They leaned against the wall, rubbing their shoulders against it, talking, laughing and scuffling with each other, their bags at their feet. There were no windows at this point in the corridor. The only things to look at were the white pipes of different thicknesses on the walls above the doors of the Home Economics rooms. The longer they waited for Mrs. Brooks, the noisier they became.

After almost fifteen minutes, Mrs. Brooks came out of the other Home Economics room, shook her head and her finger, and told them to go in quietly and sit down. Then she went back into the other room.

The class shoved into the room, jamming the doorway until some of them succeeded in fighting their way through. They went to their different units and sat for a while, but when Mrs. Brooks didn't come, they began to wander over to other tables, and talk to their friends. Some linked arms and went round and round, looking at all the posters on the walls. Chasing games started, with the accompanying screams and laughter. They were even noisier than they had been in the corridor.

Sharon was breathless with boredom; it was like a weight on her lungs. She'd looked at all the posters, and each one gave her a feeling of irritated repulsion. Cooking! It wasn't as if Brooks ever taught them anything useful, such as how to clean fish or cook a joint of meat. Part of an agent's training, before being parachuted into Norway to lead the Resistance, had been how to live off the land, and how to cook what they caught. . . All Brooks ever taught them was how to make cakes and puddings, mostly out of tins and packets, and how to make food look pretty. "Have pretty dishes you can take from oven to the table, gels, and use pretty mats and napkins. Half the appetite is in the eyes, remember." Not if you were soaked to the skin and half-starved in a turf-shelter in the Norwegian mountains, it wasn't. Sharon hated cooking as much as she hated sewing. This school was supposed to have equality for boys and girls. When they'd been at the Annexe, as first-years, the boys had learned cooking, but the girls had never learned woodwork properly. They'd just messed about in the woodwork room. And now, in the second year, at main school, it was "girls for cooking and sewing, boys for woodwork and metalwork".

Three girls were sitting on the windowsills, looking down into the yard. One of them said, "Hey, look — there's that tall feller again." Other girls crowded into the units, craning to see into the yard.

Crossing it was a young man. His height and his scruffiness were the two immediately noticeable things about him. He was over six feet tall, with disproportion-ately long arms and legs. The jeans he wore were grubby and had lighter patches on the knees and upper thighs, but they weren't at all stylish: they were plain, heavy-denim working trousers, made to last a long time. Over them he wore an old, dark blue anorak which was too short for him, and had no shape left. The bottom hem belled out round his hips, and the shoulder seam had split. Wisps of kapok fluttered from it.

One of the girls kneeling on the draining-board rapped on the window and waved. The man looked away and continued across the yard, his hands in his pockets. "Rude," the girl said, and they all agreed. He ought to have smiled and waved back.

Someone else said, "Isn't that your brother, Mary?"

The young man passed out of sight round the corner of the building, and they all turned from the windows to see which Mary had been spoken to. There were three Marys in the class. Mary Ullman, a tall, bony, gawky girl, slipped down from the draining-board, and crossed the room to her table. When someone asked again if the man in the yard was her brother, she nodded her head quickly, and then opened her text-book and stared at it in a way that suggested she didn't want to talk about him. But Mary Ullman was dopey, everybody knew that.

"What's his name, Mary?" A crowd of interested girls gathered round her table.

"Jonathan."

The girls pushed one another out of the way, leaned elbows on her table, leaned on her stooped back, and said that Jonathan was a nice name. "How old is he?"

"I don't know," Mary said.

"Don't know how old your own brother is? You're stupid."

"He's tall, isn't he?" Joanne asked. "How tall is he?"

"I don't know!" Mary felt bullied and threatened. Strands of her hair were beginning to stick to her hot face.

"What's he here for, Mary?"

"Has he come to do the drains?"

"Has he come to do the Head?" Sharon asked, and everyone laughed, a sudden, loud sound close around her, that made Mary wince.

The door opened, and Mrs. Brooks came in. Everyone rushed for their seats, especially Sharon, who was afraid that her last remark might have been overheard by the teacher.

Mrs Brooks paused just inside the door, until everyone was seated and quiet. Then she said, "But what's this, gels? Why aren't you working? What is all this laughing?"

They looked at each other guiltily, and some tried to hide their faces in their arms.

"Shrieks," Mrs. Brooks said. "Sharon. Shrieks of laughter, like a nasty hyena. Dreadful!" Girls sniggered and turned to look at Sharon. "I have never heard anything so awful. Do you always laugh like that, Sharon?"

Sharon pulled a face, behind her hand, at Joanne.

"You won't attract nice young men with sports cars if you bray like a donkey when they make a joke," Mrs. Brooks said, and made the class roar at her clever words. "Try to be quieter, my lamb." Sharon's face was as red and damp as Mary's had been a few minutes before. She hated Mrs. Brooks so much, it made her feel sick. "Have you finished the work I set you?" the teacher asked.

Someone said that she hadn't set them any work to do.

"I did!" She looked behind her. "Oh! — the board must have slipped round!" She spun the board round to reveal the numbers of pages they were to read, and of questions they were to answer. "And none of you have done any of it. Oh, you lambkins." Most of the class laughed and wriggled with pleasure at being called lambkins. Sharon was disgusted.

They got out their books and began work, though the giggling and whispering went on. Mrs. Brooks went into her store cupboard and spent some time in there, singing to herself. She came out, still singing, carrying a tray covered with a white cloth and set with a bowl of sugar and a plate of biscuits. She asked one of the girls to open the door for her, and went out. They all knew she was going to the Home Economics room next door, to prepare the little tea-party which the Home Economics and Needlework teachers held every break, together with a few other women teachers. 'Gels' talk' Mrs. Brooks called it, making Sharon feel sick every time.

She didn't even manage to finish the set reading before the end of the lesson, because it was so boring. It was about the things you could put on the floor of a house — carpets, lino and that. Trying to force herself to read it felt much the same as banging her forehead repeatedly on the spread pages of the book. She had to keep making herself begin again. God! She hated Home Economics.

Mags Firth had taught two lessons at the main school, and had driven down to the Annexe at break, where she had snatched a cup of coffee and taught two different classes in one of the rooms made by dividing the hall into three with folding doors. Next door there had been a music lesson, as there always was, since the piano was in that room. At every wail from the singers, her own class had broken into giggles. It had taken a lot out of her. She hadn't noticed it at the time, but now, walking up the steps of main school, she felt exhausted.

As she went into the entrance hall, Mr. Kendle, the

Deputy Head, was just leaving his office. The school was short-staffed, and he had actually been doing some regular teaching. The day before he had grilled her about some work-sheets he wanted, that should have been in the Resource Centre, but which he hadn't been able to find. Hadn't she agreed to keep Resources in order? She had pointed out that she wasn't being paid any extra for organizing Resources as well as teaching; but then she had meekly stayed behind after school to look for the work-sheets. She'd found them after a few minutes' search, and had put them away in a cupboard for him, meanwhile thinking of all sorts of smart cracks she could have made about 'easy work-sheet teaching'. Or perhaps a seemingly innocent question such as 'Do you really think that work-sheets do much more than keep the children quiet?' would have been a better way of getting back at him. Now she thought that she would go across, tell him where to find the work-sheets, and suggest that if he had looked just a little harder, he would have found them himself.

Before she could, a startling figure shoved through the double doors closing off the corridor directly opposite her. Big, was the word that sprang to mind. As he came through the doors he had to duck. A young man, rushing along, making the old, shapeless, torn anorak he wore bell out round him. Mr. Kendle called out, "Well, well, well! Jonathan Ullman, as he lives and breathes!"

The tall young man turned his head slightly, and gave Mr. Kendle a brief and haughty glance. He did not pause in his stride, but Mr. Kendle hurried across the tiles to get between him and the doors, "Don't run away, Ullman; don't run away."

Ullman stopped, and Mr. Kendle stood in front of him, his arms folded. He was a thin man, not particularly tall, and he looked small beside Ullman. "How are you, Jonathan?" he asked.

Jonathan hunched his shoulders, looked away across the

entrance hall for a moment, as if a shelf of potted plants were more interesting than Mr. Kendle; and then stood with his head on one side, looking down sideways at the Deputy Head with sullen contempt.

"What are you doing now?" Mr. Kendle asked. "Don't tell me *you're* on the dole, Ullman; surely not *you* ?"

God, Mags thought, you can be a swine, Kendle. Now if he puts one on you, it'll be the police, and the violence of modern youth, and you'll have asked for it.

"May I at least ask what you're doing here?" Mr. Kendle said.

Ullman swung his head round to look at the entrance hall again, and then surprised both Mr. Kendle and Mags by speaking. "What's that matter to you?"

"It matters to me because it's my duty to ask all strangers in the school what they're doing here."

"I'm fetching some fags for Kahna," Ullman said.

"What? You're fetching some — 'fags' for whom?"

"Kahna."

"Mr. Kahn, do you mean, Ullman? You may have left this school, and you may consider yourself to be a very big man out in the world, but I still think that Mr. Kahn is deserving of some respect from you."

With emphatic flatness, Ullman replied, "Kahna's the only teacher in this school I ever had any respect for."

"Shall we go and see the Head, Ullman?" Mr. Kendle said.

Ullman took a step round him. "You can, if you like."

"I want you to come with me."

Ullman paused with his back against the swing doors, gave Mags one quick, nervous, glance, and went out backwards, shoving the doors open with a thrust of his legs and bending at the waist to bring his head safely under the lintel. Once through the door he spun round and almost ran away down the steps, while the door banged shut behind him.

Mr. Kendle took a sneaky look round, and was not pleased to see Mags standing nearby, having overheard. She quickly went up to him and told him where she had put the work-sheets. Under the circumstances she did not tell him that he could easily have found them for himself. Then she went to the dining-hall and he went to the Head's office.

The dining-hall was packed. Mags joined the queue of teachers and children at the serving hatch, paid for her meal and found an empty table. Once she was seated there, all the other places at it remained empty. It was supposed to be an informal, mixed dining-hall, but the children would rather carry their plates across the corridor into the music-studio, where tables had also been set out, than sit with teachers. Jenny Griffiths soon came and sat opposite her, and they hadn't finished their first course before Mags saw Mr. Kendle edging his way between crowded tables, looking for somewhere to sit. She waved to him, and beckoned him to their table, because she was curious about Jonathan Ullman, and wanted to find out what had been decided about him in the Head's office. Jenny Griffiths looked alarmed. Like most of the junior staff, she was a little afraid of Mr. Kendle.

He sat down at the end of the table, between them, and Mags let him eat a couple of mouthfuls before asking, "Who *was* that in the entrance hall?"

Mr. Kendle took his time in answering. "An ex-pupil of mine." His voice became tighter and angrier. "It seems that he has ingratiated himself with our Headmistress, and has her full permission to roam loose about the school. The poor boy has so much experience of rejection that we must all try to give him the positive experience of being useful. It will do him so much good." Mr. Kendle pulled a face. "Claptrap! I don't know why Ullman is here, but it isn't to make himself useful, and so our Headmistress will discover if she continues to allow him to treat the school as a home from home."

"I don't know," Mags said, giving Jenny an amused look across the table. "I think it sounds rather a good idea."

"Oh yes, I know. I know why Ullman is unemployed too, the poor boy. Because he's unemployable. He's one of *those* types — never could see why he should do anything he didn't want to do. A real little classroom lawyer. If I was an employer, I know I wouldn't touch him with a bargepole."

"I don't know much about *those* types, I'm afraid," Mags said.

"Oh no, we're much too good a little *Guardian*-reading liberal to recognize a troublemaker when we see one, aren't we?" Mr. Kendle said, with the effortless rudeness that Mags considered his one real talent.

She refused to be upset. "I teach a girl named Mary Ullman. I wonder if she's related. She's not a trouble-maker."

"What year is she, first? Second? Wait until she's in the third or fourth . . . Ullman was always *quiet* — disobedient, surly, insolent, a troublemaker. The truth is, he's one of those people who're so insignificant and talentless that they've got to make themselves noticed at any price."

"Really?" Mags said. She thought that the description fitted Mr. Kendle, but before she could put this to him, he said,

"He was always a sullen, surly, thoroughly unpleasant boy, and how he's grown into a sullen, surly, thoroughly unpleasant young man."

Mags looked across the table to see if Jenny had finished. She had, and looked as if she couldn't wait to get away. They exchanged a look and rose together. As they left the room, Mags said, "Cane 'em, flog 'em!"

"I don't know how you can talk to him like that," Jenny said. "I know that's silly, but . . . You know this person you were talking about, this Ullman? Is he a very tall — ?"

"He *is* very tall," Mags said. "Why?"

"Well . . ." They reached the staffroom and went in.

27

Jenny followed Mags across to the filthy sink at the back of the room, where the electric kettle, cups and coffee-jars were kept, in a morass of coffee-grounds and tea-bags. As Mags made them both a cup of coffee, Jenny talked, and Mags kept looking swiftly from her face to what her own hands were doing. "I was teaching in the entrance hall this morning," Jenny said, "and — I think it must have been Ullman — he came along — and there were a few empty seats, you see. So he sort of — he sat down and joined my lesson." Mags looked up, her face questioning. "I thought of telling him to — clear off, but . . . I didn't know who he was, and I thought, well, I'm teaching thirty, I may as well teach thirty-one . . ."

You were too scared to tell him to go away, in other words, Mags thought.

"He was quiet most of the time . . . I was teaching about the Minoans, you know — the bull-leaping and Theseus. "Then — it was funny really," Jenny said, trying to be amused about it. " — towards the end, when the children were writing, he started asking all these awkward questions. He said, why was I teaching them a lot of fairy-tales about bull-leapers when I could have been teaching them about why Northern Ireland and Palestine are partitioned?"

"And did you tell him you were teaching the syllabus?" Mags asked.

"Oh no — I didn't think of that . . . I said the children were only twelve, and wouldn't understand about things like that —"

"Which is quite true," Mags said.

"He said anything could be explained if you used language simple enough."

"Oh yeah? Has he tried? Isn't that just like someone who's never done any teaching?"

Jenny, more at ease now she found Mags sympathetic, went on, "We got into a bit of an argument . . . I know I

28

shouldn't have, but . . . I tried to tell him, you know, about history giving people a sense of security — a sort of feeling that they've got a past and a future —"

"And a grasp of time, surely? That's an important part of history for lower school, isn't it? Getting an idea of ten years ago, a hundred years ago, a thousand —?"

"Yes, yes, I said that too — and he said, our future isn't coming out of Minoan Crete or Ancient Egypt — it's coming out of Palestine and Ireland and Poland — oh, and that children could get a better grasp of time from learning about those things, because they could see it in terms of their parents' and grandparents' lives . . ."

"Oh." Mags raised her coffee-mug and thoughtfully took a sip. She was thinking that Ullman obviously had more going on in his head than his size and his clothes had led her to believe.

"Of course, the children loved it — teacher being put in her place," Jenny said, with a nervous titter.

God, Mags thought, now she wants me to tell her, in ten easy steps, exactly how she should have handled the situation. Well, it was no part of her job to tell other members of staff how to do theirs. Cruelly, she turned her back on Jenny and said, "Let's go and sit down. I'm dying for a rest . . ."

3

Kamla had been to the dentist to have a tooth filled. The filling itself didn't bother her, but she'd been given a cocaine injection, and that did. She really preferred not to have any anaesthetic for a filling. The dentist had found it difficult to push the needle into her gum; and it had hurt, and she was sure that it would hurt a lot more when the cocaine wore off. The dentist had been white — a pleasant enough man, but she couldn't help wondering — would he have been more careful about the injection if she'd been a white girl? No, of course not — but, on the other hand, some white people had beaten up one of her neighbours the year before, for no reason — except that he was Asian. White people were all too capable of things like that, so why was it unreasonable to think that the dentist had been careless because she had browner skin than his?

But look at it this way, Kamla, she said to herself. You're going to be a doctor one day, and when you are, will you be less careful about your treatment of white people than others? Of course not . . . But then she wondered. Doctors were overworked and often tired. Might it not seem more worth while making an effort for people like herself than for people who were white and might well be despising her even as she tried to help them?

As she entered the school again, she gave herself an

30

irritable shake, trying to throw off these thoughts. It didn't help to slip into that way of thinking. She had to try to keep a balance, she had to fight for it. She didn't hate all white people because they were white, though she couldn't help noticing that they *were* white. Barbara Jones was a likable girl, and very different from Cherie Reed. Mr. Palermo was a nice, friendly man, and very different from Mr. Kendle — and she had nothing against Mr. Kendle except that he wasn't friendly. So it just wasn't *reasonable* to suppose that each and every white person she saw was hating her . . . It just seemed that way a lot of the time.

Oh, why did she have to be subjected to this backward and forward friction over every little incident? It was so wearying. She wished, like her mother, that they had stayed in Bangladesh, where it wouldn't have been necessary, where they wouldn't have had to fear bricks being thrown through their windows; where she wouldn't have been spat at in the street. True, there had been a war; but their relatives in Bangladesh had come through it without much loss. Her father always said that living standards and education were better here, but Kamla often wondered if he wasn't being a bit old-fashioned about that. England wasn't paved with gold and never had been — and she had been very happy in Bangladesh. They'd lived in a big house with her grandparents, and there had always been cousins for her to play with. She could remember a beautiful orchard where they had grown coconuts and mangoes as well as apples, and fields and fields of white flowers — at least, she thought she could remember them. The pictures in her head might actually have been put there by her mother's stories — but they were vivid.

She hadn't wanted to leave to go to England. She hadn't known her father well then. Children forget people quickly unless they see them every day, and she hadn't seen him for a long time, for months. Her mother had gone on ahead to Bombay without her because she had begged and begged to

31

be allowed to stay at home one more day, and travel to Dacca with her uncle, who was taking some of their luggage. All the grown-ups had laughed and said, "Oh, Kamla is so fond of her uncle" — and she had been, but her real reason for wanting to travel with him was that she hoped she could somehow evade her mother and return home with him. But she'd underestimated her mother's attachment to her, and she had been carried on to the plane in her mother's arms. She'd cried and cried; she could remember that. Her mother had told her how she had tried to distract her by pointing out seat-belts and flashing lights; how another passenger had taken off a charm bracelet and dangled and jingled it; how the stewardess had come and talked to her; but nothing, nothing, had stopped Kamla crying but exhaustion. Kamla could remember that clearly; and her conviction that she was being taken to a country in the sky, where there would be nothing to stand on, and she would fall and fall . . . Children have strange ideas.

Art was the last lesson of the day. She stood outside the Art-room door for a moment before going in. She enjoyed her Art lessons, but she would have enjoyed them more if Cherie Reed had not been a part of them. She ignored Cherie and, these days, Cherie ignored her; but just knowing that Cherie was there, watching her, pleased when she did something clumsy or careless, made her tense.

She went in, and Cherie was already at her desk, watching her as she crossed to hers. Mr. Kahn was sitting at one of the class desks with his friend, Jonathan Ullman. She went over to them and apologized to Mr. Kahn for being late for his lesson. He only nodded, and went on talking to Jonathan. She found the piece of work she had been doing, and set up her desk. Her painting was an abstract design of twisted triangles, that fitted together exactly, covering the paper and leaving no space between them. Looking at it now, she wasn't sure that she liked it — or, at least, not the way she'd handled it. She was wondering whether to continue with it or not when she was distracted by the loud scraping of a chair on the floor, and looked round to see Mr. Kahn get up and cross the room. He went out of the classroom, leaving Jonathan Ullman with the large, square book of engravings they had been looking at.

Jonathan turned a page or two, then closed the book, got up and, to Kamla's alarm, came towards her. She hurriedly stepped closer to her painting, dipped a brush in water and began rubbing it on a cake of paint, though it was a colour she didn't mean to use. She just hoped that if she appeared absorbed in her work and didn't catch his eye, Ullman would keep away and not bother her. She didn't want to talk to anyone, least of all him.

But he came edging between the desks and stood behind her, looking at her painting. She could feel him standing there, so big and bulky, towering over her. She didn't like tall people. She swished the paint-brush in the water, washing off the paint she had pointlessly applied to it. His silent presence set her teeth on edge. And then he said, "That's good. I like that."

It was annoying, when she had just decided that the painting was a poor one. He was only saying it to be polite. She made no answer, still hoping that he would go away.

"You're Kamla, aren't you?" he asked next. His voice was tight and nervous, as if he was as embarrassed as she was, but was struggling against it. She told him yes, her name was Kamla. It seemed too rude to ignore a direct question.

"My name's Jonathan. Ullman. Jonathan Ullman," he said. She gave a faint shrug, her back still turned to him, and began to mix a rose shade on top of the cake of white paint. He stayed there, behind her, watching her, saying nothing. In her mind she yelled at him, Go away! Why don't you bugger off back to where you came from, you're not wanted here! She almost began to giggle at the idea of saying that to him. It had been said to her often enough.

33

From the other side of the room, Cherie was watching them. Why Ullman wanted to talk to Kamla was more than she could imagine. She shook her head, shaking all her long red hair, making it quiver and shine; and then she glanced across at Ullman again. She pulled a strand of her hair forward and twirled it in front of her face, tilting it to and fro and watching the light run along it in waves of red and gold, and imagining how beautiful the whole long mass of it must look to other people. Across the room Ullman was staring at Kamla's stupid pattern as if he were hypnotized. He must be touched in the head, wanting to talk to that stuck-up little madam.

"Kahna's a good artist, isn't he?" Jonathan said. Kamla worked on as if she hadn't heard him. She didn't like the way he called Mr. Kahn "Kahna". It was impolite. "I used to be in Kahna's class," Jonathan continued doggedly. "That metal thing up there — I made that." Kamla knew what he meant — a sculpture made of metal strips welded together. The shapes changed as you turned it round, but it seemed to be two people fighting or, perhaps, embracing — the shapes of the people ran one into the other, and there seemed no end to them. It had stood on top of the paper cupboard in Mr. Kahn's room for as long as she could remember, and she'd always thought it rather good, but she wasn't going to admit that to Ullman. She didn't look at him, or answer him, and after a long, tense silence, during which she could hear him shuffling about and sucking his teeth behind her, he breathed, "Oh well . . ." and went away at last. He crashed down on to a chair far too small for him, making it creak and wobble, opened the book of engravings and began looking through it.

The rest of the lesson was peaceful and ordinary, and Kamla became so absorbed in the problems of her painting that she forgot all about Ullman and Cherie. Mr. Kahn came back towards the end of the lesson, and sat talking to Jonathan again, in his loud voice. Kamla listened in

34

snatches. Mr. Kahn had been to Vienna with his wife, on their holidays. "Beautiful, beautiful city," he said. "Everywhere you can hear music — beautiful buildings. I shall go back and see it again. Berlin? No, no, I've never been to Berlin, and I wouldn't want to go there now, not with the Wall. . . . No, that would be too grim . . . But you must come with us when we go to Germany again, Jonathan! No, no, we'd be delighted to have you with us, really —"

When the bell for the end of lesson rang, in classrooms all over the school children stood up with a crash of chairs and desks and a yell of relief; and teachers all over the school shouted, "Sit down! That bell's for me, not you! Wait until I say you can go." And then children moaned, and there was another crash of chairs as they all sat again; while a muffled roar from the corridors outside, a banging of doors and an echoing clamour, let them know that *some* classes had already been given permission to leave, or had taken it.

Even if the teachers made a class line up and leave in single file, the corridors outside the door were packed from wall to wall with people jammed together immovably, yet all fighting to move. The noise of feet stamping on the tiles and of shouting voices bounced back from the walls, floor and ceiling, and racketed in the enclosed space until it was dizzying. Getting down the stairs was dangerous. If you were caught in the centre of the steps, you couldn't reach the handrail. The people jammed behind you were all pushing forward, and the people in front of you were all straining forward too, and gave no support, so you felt that at any moment, you were about to plunge head first down the staircase. If you were against the wall or the handrail, then you were at less risks of falling, but your ribs were bruised against the rails, and your knees against the wall or the banisters.

In the corridors, you were pummelled on the back by impatient people behind, and shoved into the people in front of you. Heads were banged together, legs were

35

kicked, feet trodden on. The best plan was to wait in a classroom until the corridors were clear or, if you were turned out of the classroom, to go into the first cloakroom you could reach, and wait there.

Sharon and Joanne were bored with the daily fights in the corridor. At the end of their last lesson they remained in their seats while their classmates punched and pushed their way through the door. When they finally left the room the mayhem in the corridors was dying down, but they sat in the cloakroom, talking, until the school was almost empty.

They got up and wandered through the corridors to their form-room, for Joanne to collect some books she needed from her desk. Joanne sat down while she went through her desk, and then she didn't want to get up. Sharon, sitting slumped on a desk nearby, didn't want to move either. The walk home was so boring. They went through the same streets, past the same houses, twice a day, day after day.

But they had to drag themselves home somehow. As a beginning, Joanne left her chair and wandered round the class, opening desks, and commenting on their tidiness or untidiness. Sharon became interested, and began to do the same from the other side of the class. They awarded points for tidiness. Sharon was enjoying this game, building a story in her head about being Her Majesty's Inspector of Desks, when Joanne suddenly became bored. She went to the front of the class and picked up a piece of chalk from the ledge at the side of the board. On the board she drew a big heart, with an arrow through it, and then wrote beside it "Jonathan Ullman" and "Shaz Walker". She looked over her shoulder at Sharon and smirked.

This was a favourite game of Joanne's, and one that Sharon found deeply offensive. She went to the board, rubbed out her own name with her fist and wrote Joanne's up instead. "That's nearer the truth," she said. Joanne simpered, and didn't deny it.

"Oh come on, let's go," Sharon said. She hated it when

Joanne had these silly fads on people.

They dawdled through the empty, yellow-tiled corridors, dragging their feet, often coming to a complete halt. The walk home was too much for them. They'd never make it. Just as they reached the doors, Miss Firth came out of the Resources Centre and said good night. "Good night, Miss," they said, and then watched her walk away down the corridor leading to the Art-wing. They both pulled faces at her back and ran out into the yard.

Before Mags Firth reached the door of the Art-room, she saw Mr. Kahn himself come out of the Pottery-room. She called to him, and he smiled, and turned back towards the room he had just left, saying, "Come and look at this."

She followed him into the Pottery-room, breathing in the lovely smell of clay and paint. Mr. Kahn was standing just inside, looking at the wall behind the door. Above the long cupboard which ran the length of the wall, something had been sketched out on the wall itself — a lot of confusing lines in a dull, yellowish colour. One vivid, curving red stripe had been painted in, while others were left unpainted. Mr. Kahn plainly expected her to admire it. Not wanting to disappoint him, she frowned and studied the lines carefully, trying to make out what they were meant to be, if anything. "It's a flag!" she said finally. There was a faint outline of a fluttering flag, and a flag-pole. The red stripe was part of the flag's design.

"Jonathan's doing it," Mr. Kahn said, rather proudly. "Oh — you don't know Jonathan, do you? Jonathan Ullman — "

"I've heard of him from one or two people," Mags said. She suddenly realized what flag it was that had been roughed out on the wall. "The Stars and Stripes!" She was surprised. The impression she had formed of Ullman was not of someone who would admire America enough to want to paint its symbol on a wall. "What does the Head think of it?"

"The Head doesn't know about it, Miss. It's my room and I think I can say what goes on the wall and wha doesn't."

Mags doubted that the Head would take that view. "Life should be spicier when she does find out . . . Look, what really came to see you about is those things you said I could have . . ."

"Ah!" He hurried past her, and out into the corridor. She followed him into the Art-room. Jonathan Ullman wa there, just zipping up his worn and grubby anorak. H started to say something to Mr. Kahn, but was cut short "Don't go for a minute, Jonny — stay there." Mr. Kahn went into the store cupboard behind his desk. Mags, with smile at Jonathan, leaned against the desk, folding he arms. Jonathan turned his back on her, and so they remained strangers, uncomfortably sharing the same few square feet of space without speaking.

Mr. Kahn came out of the cupboard carrying a cardboard box. He put it down on the desk and took from it a larg conch-shell, some pieces of lava, Polish pictures made o straw, and bottles with marbles in their necks. "Here yor are; you can have it if it's any use to you — is it?"

"Oh, yes !" They were all odds and ends, but they would fill up the display shelves of the Resources Centre very well with the help of some photographs and posters. "Thanl you."

"Pleasure." Mr. Kahn bundled everything back into the box, picked it up and handed it to Jonathan. "Now yor carry that up to Resources for Miss; there's a good boy."

"Oh no!" Mags said. "No need."

"Let him carry it. That's what these giants are for. Yor don't mind, do you, Jonny?" Jonathan shook his head. "Of course not — anyway, you should talk to him, you know Miss. Very interesting family. German."

Mags glanced at Jonathan, and saw him give Mr. Kahn very sour look, and shake his head before turning away, th box clutched high against his chest. Mr. Kahn didn't notice. "Yes — German. They came here during the war, to escape from the Nazis — isn't that so, Jonny?"

Mags turned to Jonathan again, freshly interested in him. He made no answer to Mr. Kahn's question, but only looked sulky. He probably resented curiosity about his family history, but you couldn't blame people for being inquisitive. She could see the whole story flashing through her mind: a series of tiny, bright, but blurred pictures — hiding in attics, in fishing-boats, in loaded carts; the dawn arrests, the strutting, jackbooted persecutors . . . "How exciting!" she said. Jonathan lowered his head and looked into the box he was holding, his face patient but unfriendly. She felt guilty. Maybe his story was not so much exciting as brutal, or plain sad. "Well, I'd better be going — thanks for the things." At least she wouldn't keep him waiting any more.

Mr. Kahn gave her a nod, and they left him smoking at his desk. As they walked back towards the Resources Centre, Mags kept trying out in her head various questions she could ask, to get Jonathan talking about his family. "Of course, Ullman's a German name," she said eventually.

"It's English," he said flatly.

She felt foolish and snubbed for a moment — but then remembered a girl she had known at University, whose mother had been French, and her father Greek. The girl had told her that, as a child, she had spoken three languages — French, Greek and English — but as a teenager she had become increasingly irritated with her parents for using their own languages at home. It had embarrassed her in front of her friends, and she had refused to speak any language but English. Mags found this attitude impossible to understand — as a girl, she would have given almost anything to have such interesting and romantic parents — but here was the same attitude again. Of course, Jonathan's family would be Jewish as well as German and he was probably hung up on the old anti-Semitic thing. How stupid, she thought. Everything about the Jews was so admirable: their intelligence, their resilience, their determination to keep Israel, their Promised Land; the scientists, the artists they had produced . . . If she'd been Jewish, she would never have stopped boasting of it.

They reached the entrance hall, and the door of the Resources Centre. "Thanks," she said, and took the box from him. It wasn't heavy. "I teach a girl named Mary Ullman. Is she your sister?"

He nodded in reply. "Ta-ra," he said, and turned and crossed the entrance hall. He shoved the double doors hard, making them fly wide, ducked through them and disappeared from sight behind a wing of the porch. Mags carried the box into Resources. He was an odd cup of tea, she thought. Interesting, though. She hoped that she would see more of him.

Joanne and Sharon, trying to relieve the boredom of walking home, went first into a shop to buy sweets, and then started downhill, away from their estate. They would be late in getting home, but it was better than going the same old way yet again. They had been walking for some time, when Joanne said, "Hey! There's our Jane!"

Sharon looked round and saw Joanne's elder sister, Jane, on the other side of the road. She was with another girl from the sixth year, the very pretty one with the long red hair. "Let's go with them — come on," Joanne said, and started to cross the road.

"No," Sharon said, but faintly, and Joanne didn't hear her. Sharon didn't like Jane. She was seventeen, and tall, and had the same thin, dark prettiness as Joanne, but in a much more grown-up way. It was impossible for Sharon to feel that she was a tough, practical, capable fighter when she was with Jane. Jane just looked her over, and made her feel short, fat, scruffy and silly. And the girl with Jane looked to be another of the same sort . . . But Joanne was waving to her from the other side of the road, and Sharon knew Joanne. If she didn't go across, Joanne would be angry, and quarrel with her, and Sharon was miserable during the days when she had no one to talk to, no allies. So she slowly crossed the road and slowly followed behind the other three — until Joanne waved crossly, and then she ran to catch them up.

Jane and Cherie exchanged sweet, amused glances as the two younger girls joined them. It was pleasant to be run after by admiring children, and Jane was especially glad to have the chance to play the part of Big Sister in front of Cherie, who was an only child. Cherie shook her long hair, to make it shimmer, and prepared to be mysterious, but kind; reserved and aloof, but an angel.

"Anyway," Jane said to Cherie. "What were you saying?" Joanne hopped eagerly at Jane's elbow, watching the faces of the older girls, waiting tensely for an opportunity to break into the conversation. Sharon trailed along behind, feeling unwanted and awkward and fat.

"He was dere again, all frough my Art lesson," Cherie said. She spoke in a mincing, fluting, lisping little voice that caught Sharon's attention. It was revoltingly coy, but undeniably pretty; fascinating to listen to, but so false that it made you feel ashamed to be listening. "I mean, he's paid to teach *me*." Cherie pronounced the word "me" in a soft squeak, which both apologized for her existence and boasted of it. Shaz grimaced. "But he spent all his time talking to dis fwiend of his — and to *Kamla*."

"Oh, he would, to *her*," Jane said. "Well, she's a darkie, isn't she? Got to be nice to them or they'd all be up in arms."

"The Art cwass!" Cherie said. "You should be gwad you didn't take Art after all, Jane — I'm the onwy Engwish person there!" Jane gave her a surprised look, and she explained. "Well, Kamla's a — you know — And Mr.

41

Kahn's a Jew — and his fwiend that he spends all his time talking to — he's a Jew too."

"I didn't know Mr. Kahn was a Jew."

Cherie nodded her head solemnly, widening her eyes and sucking her mouth to a little rosebud to emphasize how serious she was. "Mrs. Bwooks told me so."

Joanne and Sharon looked at each other, both of them puzzled. Neither of them was really sure what a Jew was. They both knew Mr. Kahn, and they'd never noticed anything odd about him. Sharon had an idea from somewhere that it had something to do with religion, but she didn't know exactly how, or why . . . Anyhow, from the way Jane and Cherie were using it, it obviously meant something bad . . .

"He's a weal old Jew," Cherie said. "He's smelly — and he's always smoking little stub-ends. He's howwible." She shuddered. "And Jonafan Ullman is just a big, dirty lout."

"Jonathan Ullman?" Joanne said, delighted at being able to force her way into their talk at last. Sharon felt ashamed of her for being so eager. "I know who you mean — we've seen him, haven't we, Shaz? You know — Jonathan Ullman — in the yard — in Home Economics."

"Oh, shut up, Joanne," Jane said, and glanced at Cherie, hoping that Cherie had noticed the good-natured yet weary tone she had used to her little sister.

"His sister's in our class," Joanne said. "Mary Ullman."

"They're *everywhere*," Cherie said. "With them and the — well, the darkies —" She gave her hair a therapeutic shake after being obliged to use this word. "— I'm no supwised that Engwand's in twouble. . . . They just wan to take, take, take . . . My mother knew a woman who worked for some once — Jews — in a jewellery firm. Do you know what they were doing?"

"No. What?"

"They were sending gold to their friends on the Continent." Conscious that she was now talking politics which was very grown-up, she suddenly dropped her lisp. "They were making money here, and then sending it abroad. They're not interested in England, you see. They just want to use us to make money."

Sharon had been listening carefully, but she still didn't really understand. This big girl obviously knew what she was talking about, but Sharon couldn't see why sending gold to friends on the Continent was bad. It sounded very generous to her.

Jane was bored with the whole subject, and said, "I'm going to get a new dress on Saturday. You want to come and help me choose it?"

Cherie's lisp returned at once. "Oh, yeth pwease!"

4

Kamla was walking up the school drive to the Staff and sixth-form entrance when she became conscious of someone walking close beside her, someone big. She stiffened, fearing some kind of attack, and sharply turned her head to see who it was. Jonathan Ullman said, "Hello; morning."

Kamla was relieved, and her relief outweighed the annoyance she felt at his speaking to her again when she had made it so plain that she didn't want to know him. She said, "Hello."

He walked on with her. It was a good thing, Kamla thought, that she lived so far from the school, and there was no one from her own district who could report to her parents and neighbours that she had been talking to a young white man. "You got Art today?" he asked.

"No," Kamla said, wondering why does he want to know? The answer was obvious, but she didn't want to cope with the fact that he simply wanted another chance to talk to her.

A small boy stepped into Kamla's path. He was chasing after someone else, and they almost collided — would have done, except that Kamla stopped short and drew back. The boy stopped too. He was a second or third year, a stocky, hard-faced, miniature skinhead. Staring at Kamla, he made a threatening, darting, ducking motion at her, and said,

"Don't get in my way again; hear?" Kamla stared back at him mildly, aware of his menace, but also seeing him as a half-grown, silly little boy, posing as a tough guy. He moved away, looking back at her, perhaps sensing that she didn't accept him at his own valuation. He stopped again and with another ducking movement added, "Wog. Don't you get in *my* way, wog." As he self-consciously backed away, he noticed Jonathan watching him. He had to look up a long way to Jonathan's face, and he started a little, but immediately asked, "What are you gawping at, scrag-bag? I'll put one on you in a minute." Then he looked hastily round for a friend, waved, shouted, and ran off.

"Do you have to put up with a lot of that?" Jonathan asked.

Kamla took her time answering. She didn't want to seem to be whining. If she said, truthfully, yes, quite a lot, he'd probably start accusing her of being too sensitive, of mistaking jokes for abuse. She had learned — during class discussions of prejudice, for instance — that this was the reaction of most white people. "Oh, we're only joking when we call you a wog, it's just good-humoured joshing when we call you Sambo and Black-face, you shouldn't take it so seriously." "Some of it," she said.

Jonathan followed her through the double doors into the entrance-hall. "It's getting like with the Jews."

"*Is* it?" Kamla said. As far as she was concerned, being insulted by arrogant, stupid little boys was what she had to put up with, and was nothing to do with the Jews.

"I mean, the prejudice — I mean, the way it's being stoked up and used." He was *still* following her. She had thought that going to the library to register would shake him off. "I mean, it's the same — recession, people scared — find 'em a scapegoat. . . ."

"Yes, I'm sure," Kamla said. She stepped past him and went into the library. He stood by her as she marked herself present in the register, and followed her to the table where

45

she usually sat. Other sixth formers were staring at him, wondering why he was there. At last he said, "I'll see you around," and left. She always sat with her back to everyone else, and she didn't look round. She heard him walk the length of the room, and the door open and close behind him. As soon as it closed someone behind her sang, "'I like New York in June, how about Jews?'" There was a flurry of sniggering and giggling, but no outright laughter.

Kamla was used to all the other people in the form knowing more about what was going on than she did, because they were always gossiping, and she didn't talk much to anyone. She hadn't known that Jonathan was Jewish — but for them to make that jibe, he must be. Perhaps he thought that there was a special sympathy between them because she was a wog and he was a yid. He was probably too ignorant to know that she was a Moslem. He probably thought that only Arabs were Moslem, and that she must be a Hindu. She was rather glad to have thought of that, because she could keep it in mind, and it would prevent her from ever being friendly with him.

She was glad to have this extra defence. When he had come up and started talking to her that morning, after she had been so unfriendly the day before, the idea had wriggled into her mind that he might be falling in love with her. It was silly, she knew that, but it was the sort of idea that you couldn't stop yourself having. She couldn't imagine why anyone would fall in love with her, but that was the point about love: no one knew why people loved. Even worse had been the possibility that she might fall in love with *him*. It would be terrible; apart from all the trouble with her family — and his too, most likely — it would interfere with her studying, and she had a lot of hard work and exams ahead of her.

She had some experience of how distracting falling in love could be because she had been through a couple of crushes. The worst had been on a very handsome sixth-

46

former named Bipin, when she had been in the third year. When she remembered it now, it made her feel almost ill with embarrassment. She had behaved so foolishly, looking out for him everywhere, hoping fiercely that she would see him as she went in and out of school, and always wanting to talk about him. That had been the worst part of it. She had felt compelled to find excuses to tell her mother, her sister and her friends about him, even when she had known that they saw through her and were laughing at her . . . Yet when he left school, she soon forgot him. After a week or two, she'd had to work hard to keep her feelings for him alive, by picturing his face, and vowing to herself that she would never, never love anyone else . . . But for all that her endless love had trickled away and completely disappeared. Now she remembered her feelings rather than anything about *him*. So, she reasoned, love wasn't as mysterious as everyone said. You created it yourself; and you had to work to keep it alive. She thought that she would wait for her marriage, and then create some love for her husband.

But she feared her own weakness and curiosity. The English girls were always reading love-story comics, and magazines which told them how to make themselves attractive to men. They were always discussing the affairs of their friends, how this one was making a fool of herself over some boy, but that couple were made for each other, and talking about their own boy-friends and how they were engaged and were going to marry as soon as they left school. If she was in the library, there was always someone sitting close by, and although she tried not to listen to their conversations, she couldn't shut out all of it. Despite everything, their chatter made her feel that perhaps she was missing something. She tried to argue it away, but that was like trying to talk a weed out of rooting itself.

Sharon and Joanne were in Miss Firth's English class. Sharon wrote the title *Comprehension* in her book then, having no ruler, underlined it freehand. She did it badly, tried to correct it, and only made it worse. Miss Firth said, "And I want this work done tidily for a change. No scribblings out on every line, and use a *ruler* when you underline. Anyone who doesn't will do it all again."

"Hell fire," Sharon said. Joanne turned her head to look at her. "Got an ink-rubber?" Joanne shook her head, and Sharon tilted her book to show her the messy scribbling under the title. Joanne grimaced sympathetically. "I shall have to do it all again — oh, bugger!"

"Mary's got an ink-rubber," Joanne said.

Mary Ullman was sitting alone, directly in front of Sharon, and Joanne could see the things laid out on her desk. Sharon leaned forward and shook the back of Mary's chair. Mary twisted round.

Sharon made her voice soft, friendly and pleasant. "Got an ink-rubber I can borrow, please?"

Mary said, "No," and turned round again.

Though she had never given Mary any reason to like her, Sharon was surprised at this. "You have," she said. "You have got an ink-rubber." She shook Mary's chair. "Lend us your rubber, Mary. Just for a second. Look — I've got to rub this out — look." Mary wouldn't look. "I shall have to do it all again else."

"I don't care," Mary said.

"Oh! Oh! Nice! *Why* won't you lend me your rubber?"

"Because the last time I lent you anything, I didn't get it back for three days, and I had to tell a teacher on you then."

"God, that was in the first year!" Sharon said. "Watch me with it, then, if it's so bloody precious — it's only an ink-rubber!"

"*No,*" Mary said.

Sharon then threw herself back in her chair, pettishly incensed that Mary should refuse her such a little favour. It wasn't fair. It was mean. And that connected with some new information she had picked up. Leaning forward

48

again, she shook Mary's chair and whispered, with spiteful intensity, "Jew!" Mary dragged her chair forward, tucking her legs hard under her desk, and Sharon couldn't reach her. She snatched up Joanne's ruler, which was lying near her, and poked Mary in the back with it, digging in the corners as hard as she could. "Jew — Jew!"

"Sharon — Mary. What *is* going on?" Miss Firth came slowly up the aisle, her hands on her broad hips. Sharon drew back into her seat, slyly replacing the ruler on Joanne's desk, and becoming small and meek. "What were you poking Mary in the back for, Sharon?"

Sharon looked sulkily at her desk-top, pouting and wagging her head slightly. "I only asked her to lend me a rubber, Miss, that's all, and she wouldn't."

"If that's the way you ask, I'm not surprised."

"I asked her nicely," Sharon said. "And she wouldn't." Because she's a stingy old Jew, her thoughts went on.

Miss Firth, her hands still on her hips, looked down at Sharon's book. "You should have used a ruler, shouldn't you? You'd better rule that off and start again, hadn't you?"

Sharon kept her head lowered to hide her scowling face, and thought horrible thoughts about Miss Firth. The cow. She'd never liked her. There wasn't a single thing about Miss Firth that she liked: not her accent, nor her fat backside, nor her trousers that she shouldn't wear, nor the loose tops she always wore over them, nor her speckly-framed glasses and spotty face. She was just horrible. And Sharon was going to get Mary Ullman for getting Firth on to her and showing her up in front of the class like this.

"Get on with your work now — *all* of you." Miss Firth started back down the aisle. "Let's have no more squabbles." She stopped just in front of Mary's desk, and Mary began to sweat, wondering what she'd done. "I was talking to your brother last night, Mary," Miss Firth said.

Mary hunched her shoulders, and ducked her head between them.

"He was telling me a little bit about your family. I never knew I was teaching someone so interesting. What part of Germany do your people come from?"

"I don't know, Miss," Mary said, resenting the inquiry. She could feel the pull of listening ears all round her. Everyone was wondering what was so special about her, and being jealous. She was hardly the most popular person in the class anyway; why was Miss Firth making things more difficult for her? What had she done to Miss Firth?

Miss Firth, realizing that Mary was unwilling to talk, smiled vaguely and went on down the aisle to her desk. As soon as the teacher was settled, the girl in front of Mary turned round. "What's your family done, then?"

The boy across the aisle whispered, while watching Miss Firth, "Is there somebody famous in your family?"

Mary, her mouth tightly closed, her face lowered and hidden, shook her head fast: no, no, no. Leave me alone.

From behind her came other whispers. "Kraut," Sharon said. Sharon was happier with this insult, knowing exactly what it meant: 'Krauts' were the people the Resistance had fought, the people Natalie had machine-gunned, and if Mary was a Kraut, that was a good enough reason to hate her. "I'm going to get you, Kraut." Mary wouldn't look round and was pretending that she didn't hear, so Sharon used the ruler again, jabbing it into her back. "Kraut. Jew. I'm going to get a gang on to you, at break, Jew-Kraut. I'll learn you. You won't show me up again."

The bell rang for break. Mr. Kendle was crossing the yard, on his way to his office from the mobiles, when he saw a crowd of children pressing against one of the windows in the Art-block. He came up quietly behind them, and peered through the glass to see what was interesting them so much.

It was the window of the Pottery-room. Directly opposite him as he looked through the window, painted on the wall, were bright red, curving stripes. In one corner was a patchy blue square. The children, noticing him, began to edge away, and he was about to leave himself when he saw Jonathan Ullman enter the Pottery-room from the corridor. Ullman picked up a tube of paint and brush, staring insolently at Mr. Kendle through the glass. Climbing on a chair, he began painting on the wall. Mr. Kendle stayed a little longer, watching him. Such unauthorised daubing on the fabric of the school would not go down well with the local authority, and what didn't go down well with them would frighten the Head. He went off to find her. It was his duty to tell her what was going on, but it gave him a lot of pleasure too; pleasure that he didn't try to hide. In his opinion, the school had gone from bad to worse since the old Head had left. The new one believed all the nonsense trotted out as sociology, and could be sweet-talked by any bovver-boy.

Mags Firth was on her way to the coffee-bar when she saw Jonathan Ullman leaning against the wall at the entrance to the Science-wing. "Hello!" she said. He looked down at her and nodded. "Want a cup of coffee?"

He seemed so reluctant that she was about to shrug and pass him by, but then he said, "Yeah, okay," and joined her.

An old store-cupboard, situated at a wide bend in the corridor, had been converted into a coffee-bar. Tables and chairs had been set out nearby, and benches installed along the walls. It had been intended for the fifth and sixth years, but the more rowdy among them had been banned and shut out of the school with the younger children at break; and the younger and less conventional members of staff had taken to going there for their coffee instead of to the staffroom, with the result that few pupils used the place at all.

"I'll get the coffee," Mags said, as soon as they went through the fire-doors into the coffee-bar. Ullman didn't protest, or make any offer to pay, and she felt piqued, even

51

though she would have refused his offer if he had made it.

Carrying their spilling cups, they made their way between chairs and over people's legs to an empty corner of the wall-bench. Mags was trying to think of a leading question which would lead Jonathan to pour out his family's entire history, especially the part about escaping from the Gestapo. She couldn't think of any polite way to ask. So, when they did sit, she only said, "What a morning I've had!" He set his cup of coffee on the point of his knee, holding it there and studying it. Stains of muddy water spread over his jeans leg.

"Well!" she said. "How long is it since you left here?"

"Five — six years."

Mags switched on her half-frowning, sincerely concerned expression. "And now you're unemployed?"

He turned towards her. "I've never had a job."

"*Never*? In five years?"

"I've had jobs — not real jobs. Temporary work. I washed lorries with cold water and washing up liquid in January — that's how I got me clothes like this." He drank coffee, staring blankly above the rim of the cup. "I haven't done anything for the past couple of years, though."

Mags had no personal experience of unemployment, but she knew well enough from the parents and elder siblings of the children she taught, and from her colleagues, that it was becoming harder and harder to find a job. Despite this, she wondered if Ullman had *really* tried. "You've been to dozens of interviews, then?" she said.

He reached inside his anorak and took out a square of crumpled, grubby, folded paper. Mags took it and unfolded it carefully; it was worn along the creases. The two sheets of foolscap paper were covered with writing. Some badly made, ugly letters read, "Monday August 6th, Nettles Light Engineering". Underneath, in a different hand-writing were the words, "No vacancies" and a signature she couldn't read. Another entry in the bad, clumsy lettering followed: "Monday August 6th, Shepherd's Tools Ltd.," and then, "Mr. Ullman called at our firm on the above date asking for employment but we regret that we have none to offer at the present time," and another signature. Entry after similar entry covered the sheets.

"Social Security asked me where I'd been for jobs and I couldn't remember," Jonathan said. "I go round factory estates, asking. I don't look at the names. They said, if I couldn't remember, maybe I hadn't been doing any looking. So I took paper with me and collected that lot. Then they said, oh good, at least we got you out looking . . . So I thought, right, if that's the name you've given me, I won't bloody look. So I come here."

"Back to the scenes of your happiest days?" Mags said.

"I hate this place. I'd have got a job when I left if it hadn't been for this place."

Mags thought this extreme, even allowing for the way people generally felt about their schools. "How's that?"

"I wanted to be a sheet-metal worker when I was a kid. I dunno why. I just decided on that. I wanted to take metal-work in the fourth year — you know, when they start dishing out the career advice. Only the metal-work class was overbooked, so they started in on me. 'You're bright, Jonathan, you can do better than that if you pull your socks up.' All that stuff. And dear old Mutti and Vati lap it up, don't they? So I get shunted into O-levels. The only metal-work I got to do was what Kahna tried to teach me."

"How many O-levels did you get?" Mags asked.

"I dunno. Two or three, I forget. They're no use to me anyway . . . If I'd been left alone and done metal-work, had that bit of training, I could have got a job when I left school. It wasn't so bad then."

"Well, there are training schemes, night-schools —"

"People like you think it's so sodding easy," he said, and the thought crossed her mind that, whatever his family had been, it was possible that he was just an ill-mannered lout.

53

"I've been on every fancy-named cheap-labour election-winning scheme going, and they're all cons . . . Anyway, I don't want to be a sheet-metal worker any more. Making cabinets to somebody else's design for the rest of me life? Stuff that . . . I've changed. They could have had a happy little sheet-metal worker, but now they're stuck with me."

Mags felt obscurely guilty, just for being a teacher. She tried to defend herself against it, but Marxist maxims about the education system's sole purpose being to stamp people into the shape required by a rotten system kept whispering into her mind. Teachers are masochists, she thought. They work like dogs to do their best for everybody, but they're never happy unless they can find something to blame themselves for.

Out in the yard, Joanne and Sharon told the story of their grievance against Mary to Anita, who was as struck by the injustice of the whole affair as they were. How did Mary dare; who did she think she was; who'd ever heard of anybody being so mean? Joanne passed on the theory that Mary was mean because she was Jewish, or perhaps it was because she was German; she was, in any case, foreign, not English. Anita thought this very likely, and exclaimed in delight when Sharon proposed that they should get a gang together and get Mary, to show her. Yeah; that'd teach her; that'd put her in her place! Anita ran round the yard and found two of her friends, Carol and Diane, who were just as eager. The idea of being a member of an avenging gang, punishing the mean and unjust, was exciting and appealing.

They began to look for Mary. The yard was large and crowded, so, in order that they shouldn't lose one another and come upon Mary while alone, they linked arms and walked to and fro across the yard in a human chain. People had to move aside to allow them to pass, and their sense of importance was increased. They began to call for Mary, and turned her name into a chant: "Mary, Mary, we're going to get you, Mary!" A boy charged against Joanne's and Carol's arms, breaking their link, and running on without looking back. This shook their confidence for a moment. It seemed that not everyone was prepared to walk round them. But after a flustered second, they shouted names after the boy, joined arms again, and continued with their search and their chant.

They crossed and recrossed the yard several times, veering aside to inspect corners and dragging the rest of the tittering chain after them, growing euphoric with excitement and boasting; but they didn't find Mary.

"She's hiding," Sharon shouted. "She's hiding from us. She knows we're after her."

Joanne said that she would be in the lavatories, and they ought to go in and get her, but since it was forbidden to go into the school during break, the others weren't so keen. Carol, backed by Diane, suggested that they should look round the other side of the building: Mary might have gone there, hoping to escape their notice.

It was also forbidden for pupils to go behind the school building, where the kitchen and gym entrances were, without a teacher with them, but this rule was more easily broken. Prefects and teachers were posted at every door to prevent people going inside, but the teachers on duty in the yard were always walking about, and they could be dodged. Dragging each other along, the five girls crossed the yard in the opposite direction to the patrolling teacher and dashed round the corner of the building, laughing and giggling noisily.

They ran over a mixture of gravel and coke that slid about and crunched under their feet, and through a blast of hot, moist air from the kitchens. Ahead of them was the flight of steps from the first-floor gym; and someone sitting on the steps hurriedly ducked behind them in an attempt to hide. "There she is!" Joanne yelled. Sharon had doubted that Mary would be hiding behind the school, and to find that she was, after all, was a tremendous boost, almost an assurance that luck, and right, and justice were on their side. They cheered and ran, and swung round the steps in a rush of energy and noise, colliding with Mary, surrounding her. And then they didn't know what to do.

They had intended to hit Mary, to teach her that, in future, she should lend Sharon a rubber whenever she asked; but with Mary close enough to hit, and no one to stop them hitting her, they suddenly found it hard to nerve themselves to do it. Mary expected them to hit her, and cringed away, hunching her shoulders and clenching her fists up near her face, but though the sight of her cowardice made Sharon feel both angry and disgusted, it didn't make it any easier to hit her.

"Hiding!" Joanne said, and pushed Mary into the treads of the steps behind her. "You were hiding, weren't you? Thought you'd get away with it, didn't you? Well, you were wrong! 'Cos you're stupid — you couldn't hide from — you couldn't hide from a *badger!*" As she spoke, Joanne kept pushing Mary and giving her little slaps and pokes, and she kept glancing at Sharon with a smile, inviting Sharon to admire and appreciate what she was doing. None of the pokes or slaps was very hard, but Mary began to grizzle, from fear, and from the pain of being disliked and bullied.

"Cry-baby!" Sharon said. "What you snivelling for? We haven't touched you yet!"

"Cry-baby Kraut!" Joanne said cleverly, and her face was bright with pleasure and excitement when everyone — except Mary — laughed. "Cry-baby Jew!" she cried, but that didn't go down as well. No one seemed to notice. Joanne punched Mary on the arm to relieve her disappointment.

Carol reached over Joanne's shoulder, took a strand of Mary's hair and began to pull and twist it, tugging Mary's hair down. "You shouldn't have tried to get out of it. You're going to get it twice as bad now for that. You should

56

just have took your punishment properly."

"Yes," the others agreed.

"Shazzer only wanted to lend your rubber for a few minutes," Joanne shouted in Mary's contorted face as Carol held her head down by her hair. "That's what you get for being so mean, you Jew!" And she punched Mary on the back.

There was a gasp, and then an outbreak of giggling at this, the first real blow to be struck. Diane backed away from them slightly and watched, smiling, from a short distance. But the other four felt a sense of release. Now Joanne had started, they could join in. "She called you a thief an' all, didn't she, Shaz?" Carol asked, and gave Mary's head a vicious downward tug.

"Yeah, she did." Sharon was eager now to show that she was the toughest of all of them. She took Mary's ears and looked into her face, though Mary wouldn't look back. "I didn't steal your cruddy rubber and you shouldn't have said that I did, because I don't forget things like that, and I don't let people get away with saying things like that to me." Spoken slowly and impressively, it was too powerful a speech to follow merely with a slap or a push. There was a moment's hesitation while Sharon pondered what to do, and then she banged Mary's head on the wooden step behind her. There was a loud crack, louder than Sharon had expected; and Mary gave a howl of pain, slapped her hands to her head, and then began to sob with a soft, hissing noise, and spasms which shook her body and doubled her over.

Sharon stepped away from her. She hadn't planned to bang Mary's head like that; it had just flashed into her mind and she had done it. The noise, and Mary's howl, had frightened her. Maybe she'd fractured Mary's skull, and she would die! She twisted round to look behind her, fearing that a teacher was creeping up, and then ran away, back to the yard, trying to get as far away from Mary as possible, so that when Mary was found, sobbing, she wouldn't be associated with her. The other four ran after her. They began laughing again, giggling with a mixture of fear, excitement, and the sheer exhilaration of running so fast. They ran round the corner of the building and right across to the other side of the yard before they stopped and let themselves drop breathlessly on to the low wall. They were hot, damp with sweat, their hair untidy; and they were stretched, tired and happy. It had been a wonderfully lively and entertaining fifteen minutes, instead of the usual dreary hanging about the yard.

"That showed her," Carol said, almost too breathless to get the words out.

"She should be taught a really good lesson," Joanne said. "What if we get her again tomorrow?"

They smiled and nodded, looking forward to another exciting break from lessons the next day; and, at the same time, feeling strong and good, even noble. They were doing right, correcting a naughty girl in her misguided course, just as their parents and teachers corrected them when they went wrong.

Mary, left alone, sat on the dusty concrete to cry. She was hurt, afraid, ashamed, and desolately unhappy. Why was she such a coward? Why hadn't she stood up to them? Why did everyone hate her so much? Why did they pick on her when they didn't pick on anyone else? She cried until she had no breath left and her ribs hurt, until her face was wet and dirty, and her hair stuck to it in a net. By that time, break was over, and she had to sneak in by a side door. She went into the nearest girls' lavatory and locked herself into a cubicle, and there, sitting on the lavatory's lid, she told herself all her troubles until she began to cry again. There wasn't anybody else she could tell. Her parents would say, look after yourself, and if she told on Sharon and the others to a teacher, they would get her again. She wished she were dead.

58

Sharon and Joanne noticed her absence from the lesson, and laughed over it, though when it occurred to them that Mary might have gone to the Head — or died — they were worried. But they were relieved of that fear when Mary came into the next lesson, peeping at them from the corners of her eyes in an obviously cowed manner. They grinned and pointed at her when the teacher wasn't looking, and Sharon mimed the action of someone being hanged before falling over her desk and giggling with Joanne.

At the end of the afternoon, Mags Firth hurried into the staff-room, collected some books, and had turned to go before noticing Jenny Griffiths among the members of staff sitting round a coffee-table. "Jenny — want a lift? You'll have to come right away."

Jenny stood. "I've just got to get — "

"I'll see you at the car," Mags said, and, calling a general goodnight to everyone, she left.

Jenny came running down the steps from the school a few minutes later, clumsily carrying her bag, her coat, and several books. Mags opened the door, and she clambered in, throwing the bag and coat on to the back seat.

"How's today been?" Mags asked, as she turned on the ignition.

"Oh, not too bad, not as bad as yesterday . . . We were just talking about that Ullman man again — do you know he's painted a huge mural on the wall of the Pottery-room?"

"Oh, yes . . . It's an American flag."

"No — it's a Russian flag."

"I've seen it," Mags said. "It's the Stars and Stripes."

"Oh," Jenny said. "I'm sure Mr. Kendle said it was a Russian flag. He reported it to the Head — "

"Oh, he *would*!" Mags said irritably.

"The Head's not doing anything about it, anyway," Jenny said. "She told Mr. Kendle that to make a fuss about it now would be to give it more importance than it

warranted, and she thought it would be better to ignore it."
Jenny laughed. "Mr. Kendle said that was typically wishy-washy and just what he expected of our Head."

"What Mr. Kendle dislikes about the Head's decision is that she got the job instead of him, and she's a woman."

"She is a bit soft, though, isn't she? . . . Well, from what I've heard," Jenny said. "I've got to admit . . . I think that sort of job *is* better done by a man — don't you, really?"

"*What?*" Mags said, but the word came out weakly, astonishment causing her voice to fail, and Jenny ran on.

"Anyway, round this American flag, or Russian flag, or whatever it is, he's written up political slogans." She spoke in a tone of deep disapproval.

"Dear, dear," Mags said. "What do they say?"

"Oh, I'm not sure — I haven't seen it. This is just what Mr. Kendle was telling us."

"Ah. It'll be something left-wing, then, if *he* calls them 'political' in that voice-of-doom. The Tories aren't political, you know. They just are."

"But we're not allowed to put up political things in schools, are we?" Jenny said. "Schools aren't supposed to teach politics."

"Don't you think they should?"

"Oh, I don't know," Jenny said, in a tone which meant that she was thinking about it very fair-mindedly, but actually thought that they shouldn't be taught in schools under any circumstances. "*Any*way, Ullman has been making himself an awful nuisance — people were saying — he went into house-assemblies — "

"My *God!*" Mags exclaimed.

"No, but Mags — he's a disruptive influence. I mean, the children keep looking at him and nudging each other and giggling — "

"Yes, I know, I know," Mags said.

"He shouldn't be in the school, whatever you say. He makes it more difficult for the teachers."

60

Mags glanced at her. "Shouldn't *you* have all the way-out views? Why are the young so staid these days? The kids I teach — they're all right-wing, reactionary, repressive, conformist, every one. I was discussing with some fourths — " She paused as she swung the car round a corner. "Should hanging be brought back? I asked them. It was unanimous — yes. For murder, terrorism — and rioting. I said — I should have known better than to be sarcastic — but I said, 'How about chopping off hands for stealing while we're on?' Oh yes! they said. Wonderful idea. They all agreed on it — even one who I know, for certain, is on probation for stealing a car."

She glanced at Jenny again, and Jenny smiled and shook her head indulgently, without bothering to say that she thought hanging should be brought back for murder and all serious crimes of violence, and that the police should be armed too. She knew that Mags wouldn't sympathize.

Kamla stayed in the library until ten minutes or so before her bus was due. As she approached the gate she saw Jonathan Ullman sitting on the wall. Oh no, she thought, and pretended not to have seen him. She told herself that he probably wasn't waiting for her anyway; it was big-headed to think that he was.

But as she passed him, he got up and began to dawdle along behind her. The muscles of her back tightened. If someone who knew her saw her walking and talking with this man, and it got back to her parents, she would be in trouble . . . But, of course, he didn't know that. In her head she started chanting, Go away, go away, go away.

He said, "Hello." He sounded too off-hand and casual, betraying how carefully he had rehearsed this. She shifted her gaze a little further from him and said nothing. He forgot his script and, with some annoyance, said, "Look; you don't mind me talking to you, do you?"

She thought of saying, 'yes', but politeness and a certain

61

pleasure in being waited for and courted made her weaken and say, "No."

"It seems like you're the only intelligent person in the whole bloody school," he said.

She abruptly crossed the pavement to the road, cutting in front of him and making him stop short. As she paused at the kerb, she said, "I have a bus to catch." Did he think she was stupid enough to fall for such flattery? They had hardly spoken, so how did he know how intelligent she was? She crossed the road and began to climb the hill to the bus-stop.

He still tagged along behind her. "Kahna's told me a lot about you. He likes you. He thinks you're very intelligent. He said you're going to be a doctor — is that right?"

"That all depends on whether I'm intelligent enough to get to Medical School," she snapped. She was pleased that Mr. Kahn should think her intelligent, but resented the fact that he had been talking about her behind her back.

"You will," he said. Another piece of flattery. "Most of the kids at that school are thick. And the teachers too. I've been listening to 'em these past couple of days. I've been painting in the Pottery-room — you seen it?" He paused, but she carried on walking, her head up and her eyes to the front, saying nothing. "Well, they keep coming in to have a nose, and I've been talking to 'em. They don't know anything. They've never heard of Iran. They don't know what's going on there — fourteen and fifteen years old, some of them. You'd think they'd have picked up something. They all watch television." Against her will, her interest was captured. They had reached the bus-stop, and she stood beside it with her back turned to him, apparently ignoring him, but listening carefully. "They don't know anything about Israel," he went on. "They don't know who the Palestinians are. And that — " He swung round and pointed a long arm at the building down the hill. "That's supposed to be a school."

Of course, he would want them to be taught all about

62

Israel, Kamla thought. He would want them to be taught a lot of propaganda. He wouldn't be so keen for them to know who the Palestinians were if they were taught how the Palestinians had been kicked out of their own country and made refugees by the Israelis. No, he would want them to be taught that Palestinian equalled terrorist. But even so, he *did* seem to be interested in other countries besides England, which, in her experience, was unusual . . . "They are ignorant, many of them," she said. "Some of the people in the sixth form with me don't know where Bangladesh is — or they think it is just an Indian state."

His face contracted with curiosity. "Is that where you come from, Bangladesh?"

She hesitated. If she answered, she could be drawn into quite a long conversation. She looked down the road and saw the roof of her bus, just visible over the brow of the hill, so she would be able to get away soon, in any case. "Yes," she said, proudly. "We left there when I was six."

He came closer to her, which she did not much like. "Did you have to leave because of the war?"

"Here's my bus," she said; but she thought: He knows there was a war!

She had come to expect that most English people knew nothing and cared less about India, Pakistan, Bangladesh. As the bus drew closer, she said, "No; we left before the war . . . I came with my mother — to join my father. He had been working here." She raised her head and gave his face one good look, searching it for signs that her father's working in this country, and his sending for his family, were disapproved of. Ullman didn't seem to disapprove, but perhaps he was just better at hiding his feelings than other English people.

The bus pulled up in a cloud of fumes, dust, grit and noise. She climbed on as the other people were getting off, and dropped her money into the cash-box beside the driver. She had to wait until the aisle was clear before she could collect her ticket and sit down. She looked out through the bus doors and saw that Jonathan had gone.

She sat next to the window, with an empty seat beside her. The bus chugged on from stop to stop. It passed a dress shop, and her thoughts drifted from the dresses displayed in its window to a beautiful sari she had seen in a shop near her home. It had been white, with golden mandalas made out of sequins. The mandalas were just like the swastikas the National Front used for their symbol, but the other way round. She wondered what NF members would make of a sari decorated with swastikas . . . The bus stopped again and a tall thin woman of about fifty got on, dressed in a mottled brown coat and wearing a rusty-coloured hat. She came along the aisle and paused momentarily by Kamla's seat. Kamla raised her head and smiled, and the woman, with a reaction too obvious to be natural — a mime intended for the other passengers on the bus — stepped back. She twitched her features into an exaggerated expression of horror and distaste, as if she had seen something disgusting. To make her feelings even clearer to everyone watching, she made herself shudder, and then whisked away down the aisle to another seat.

There was an unnatural silence in the bus, a sense of everyone sitting tight in their own little space, not looking at each other, keeping themselves to themselves. Kamla turned her head and looked out of the window at the rich street, with the trees flourishing in every garden, the fashionable painted gates, the pretty doors. She felt completely stunned and numb with astonishment. She didn't realize how hurt she was until tears began filling her throat and stinging in her eyes. Despite her struggle to hold them back the tears ran over her lids and down her face. She slumped closer to the window, hunching her shoulders, trying to hide her face from the other passengers. Not one of them tried to give her any sign that they did not share the woman's feelings about her. Did they all approve of what that woman had done, then? She could feel, she was sure, hostility all round her; dozens of minds silently cheering and gloating, applauding that woman and hating Kamla.

She was almost used to the silly gibes and jeers of children — children knew no better. But how could a woman so old be so callous and cruel? And how could *she* be such a fool? She had smiled at that woman.

The bus reached her stop. Kamla got off and dragged her feet along the pavement, walking slowly to give herself time to wipe away all the tears and be calm. She breathed deeply, and tried to think of something that had happened during the day that she could make into a little story to tell when she went in. A story as funny as she could make it — it didn't really matter if it was funny, so long as she appeared to find it funny, and her mother would think that she enjoyed school. She had been telling such stories for years. Her parents might read about racism in British schools in the newspapers, but they would never hear about it from her.

5

Before break there was a single Art lesson. Jonathan arrived about fifteen minutes after it started, and hardly spoke a word to Mr. Kahn before going over to Kamla. Cherie shook out her hair and watched them jealously. She felt strongly that Ullman ought to talk to her because she was not only more beautiful than Kamla, and didn't wear glasses, but she was white too. Why was he always talking to Kamla when *she*, Cherie, was in the same room? Why wasn't she getting some attention? It wasn't fair.

When Kamla saw Jonathan coming across the room, smiling shyly, she was annoyed as well as pleased. She remembered the white woman who had insulted her on the bus the day before, and how she had innocently smiled at the monster. And now here was Jonathan, smiling, expecting to be politely spoken to. Yet *he* hadn't insulted her, and she was always constrained by politeness. She often wished that she could be as callous as the woman on the bus; she'd say whatever she felt like to everyone then, and never care whom she offended or hurt.

Jonathan leaned on the cupboards beside her. "That's great," he said, ritually, of her painting. Her mouth closed more tightly. "You say you come from Bangladesh?" he asked, nervously casual, and she realized that this was why he had come to talk to her — to talk about Bangladesh. At once she felt more relaxed and more annoyed.

"No, I don't *say* - I *do* come from Bangladesh. I was born there." With a slap of her brush at a painting she was beginning to dislike strongly, she added, "Why do *you* want to know?"

"I'm interested . . . Hey, do you know much about the war with Pakistan?"

"No."

"I read that three million Bangladeshis were killed in that war," he said.

Kamla raised her brows. What was she supposed to say? She didn't know if the figure was right or wrong; it couldn't be anything more than an estimate. And why tell her? She knew much better than he that it had been a horrible, treacherous, vicious war. Three million . . . somewhere deep in her mind there began spreading a curious, cool, impersonal anger, and fear: a horror of three million dead who all belonged to her. There was nothing she could do for or about them. She took the painting from the ledge on her easel, and tossed it on to the cupboard behind her. She was sick of it; she had gone wrong with it. She closed her desk down, and sat on her chair, her arms folded.

"I read," Jonathan said, "that since the year 1900, nearly forty million people have been killed, in genocidal wars and death camps, refugee camps . . . Forty million people. And the same book said, it's been two thousand years since Christ is supposed to have saved us all, and two thousand years doesn't add up to *one* million days. But just since 1900 we've killed forty million people . . . More than that. More by now."

Kamla listened, wondering what kind of nut he was.

"That doesn't include the wars that weren't genocidal — like the First and Second World Wars, Vietnam, Korea, Northern Ireland, the Falklands . . ."

"What about the Israeli war on Lebanon?" Kamla said. "Do you count that as genocidal, or don't you? and *I* would

67

say that the Americans were genocidal in Vietnam too."

"Ah — Lebanon," Jonathan said, and reached out for a chair. Lifting it into place in the aisle beside her desk, he sat astride it. "In Lebanon —"

On the other side of the room, Cherie worked on her picture. It showed some people in old-fashioned clothes having a picnic on a lawn. She had drawn it very carefully, and was painting it slowly, with equal care, balancing the colours and choosing them carefully. She had given a lady on one side of the picture a nice lilac dress; so she gave a gentleman on the other side a nice lilac-striped blazer, to match the two sides up. Now, proud of her patience and neatness, she was painting the grass pale green all round the figures and their table-cloth.

Joanne and Sharon had been looking for Mary all over the yard. They hadn't been able to find Diane and Carol either, and Anita had grown bored and gone off. "If we don't get her now, we can get her at dinner-time," Joanne said.

Her sister Jane and Cherie came out of the school, walked delicately down the steps from the main entrance, inspected a patch of the low wall at the bottom of the steps, and sat on it. Jane had a plastic container of orange-juice with her, which she opened and passed to Cherie.

"Come on," Joanne said, and started towards them.

"Oh *no*, Joanne!" Sharon said; but when Joanne didn't stop or turn, she only tutted before trailing after her.

"Oh, for God's sake, clear off!" Jane said, when she saw Joanne. She didn't feel like showing off her little sister that day.

"I'm not coming to talk to *you*," Joanne said, and sat beside Cherie on the wall. Cherie shook back her hair and smiled at her, seeing herself as gracefully, beautifully kind to children. Voices in her head said, "She's so good with children, she really loves them; she's like an angel." Or a madonna.

68

"We've been looking for Mary Ullman — you know, she's the sister of that big bloke," Joanne said.

"Have you?" Cherie asked. Sharon, standing in front of them, thought that Cherie was overdoing the sweetness. Joanne was twelve, not two.

"We're going to get her when we find her," Joanne said, and Cherie turned to Jane with a sweet, kind, amused smile: how cute these children were! Sharon wished that Joanne would stop making a fool of them in front of these big girls — but she couldn't help admiring Cherie's prettiness and grace.

Joanne was explaining why they were going to get Mary, telling Cherie all about how Mary had refused to lend Sharon her rubber, and how Miss Firth had taken Mary's side too, and told Sharon off — for nothing!

"Oh, they always do take *their* side," Cherie said. "Don't they, Jane?"

"Bloody teachers?" Jane said. "If there's a wrong side, you can bet they're on it."

"We got her yesterday for it," Joanne said. "We got her behind the gym, and made her cry."

"Oh, goodie!" Cherie said, and looked to see if she had made Jane smile, but Jane seemed to be in a sour mood. Two black girls walked past, and Cherie turned her head so that her long red hair fell down and made a screen for her eyes between her and them — but she peeped sideways past it, and said, "There are a lot of people wound here who ought to be taken down a peg or two."

Jane, who had been thinking about something else, looked up and saw the girls. "What a stink there is round here!" she called out. One of them looked round, gave her a weary and scornful look, and walked on again.

Cherie giggled. "Oh, *Jane*!" Jane grinned, flattering herself that she had been daring and outrageous. But Cherie had become very serious. Sitting prettily on the wall, she let her simple, natural wisdom shine through. "It's not funny, though; not weally it isn't — is it? 'Cause they keep coming in and coming in, and nobody does anyfink to stop them. I think it's tewwible. We're onwy a little countwy. Somefink ought to be done to stop dem before it's too late."

A silence. Sharon saw Jane, her expression consciously serious, nod solemnly, as if Cherie was so right that there were just no words to say how right she was. Sharon was impressed. She felt that she was listening to deep talk, intelligent beyond her understanding. The silence, the nods, the unsmiling faces spoke of knowledge she could not share. She never doubted that two such beautiful, fashionable, stylish girls were grown-up, intelligent, in possession of all the facts.

Break ended, and they went back into the school, Jane and Cherie to the library and Sharon and Joanne to their next class, history. As Mr. Palermo was returning marked books, and the class were chattering, Sharon leaned close to Joanne and whispered, "We ought to start like a Resistance."

"A what?" Joanne said.

"You know — in the War, when the Germans were taking over France, they had a Resistance. All French people got together and they used to kill Germans and blow trains up and that. In secret. The Norwegians did it an' all."

Joanne stared at her. "So what?"

Sharon was impatient. "So we could be a Resistance against the darkies, of course!"

Joanne got the idea. Her eyes and mouth opened wide in delight.

"I mean, I know we can't kill anybody," Sharon said hurriedly, getting that point out of the way, "but we can do like we did to Mary." This, she had to admit, sounded tame beside the activities of the Resistance, and she waited anxiously to hear if Joanne would scoff.

"Just think — if, in all schools, all over the country,

people start doing the same," Joanne said, her face bright. "They might get to hear what we're doing, and copy us. And everybody'd be like, fighting back, because of us."

Sharon was relieved and encouraged. "Yeah! It'd be a proper Resistance . . . We'd have to have a name. The French Resistance was called 'The Mackie'."

"Let's be 'The Avengers'," Joanne said.

"No — that's too —" Not original enough. "Something like — 'Those Who Strike in Secret . . .' "

"*No!*" Joanne said scornfully. " 'The Destroyers'."

"Quiet now," Mr. Palermo called out.

"Well, we can think of a name," Sharon said hurriedly. "Let's tell Anita and them, at dinner-time."

Joanne nodded excitedly.

Sitting on the little chairs of the Art-room, facing each other across a narrow aisle, Kamla and Jonathan talked until break was over, and another class started lining up outside the door. Then they had to leave, but Kamla had the next lesson free, so they walked no further than a cloakroom at the end of the Art-wing corridor. There were benches under the coat-hooks, and they sat opposite each other again. Kamla rested her arm on her school-bag beside her, and sat neatly, legs crossed. Jonathan sat with his long legs spread — there wasn't room for them in the narrow space otherwise. One scuffed, dirty brown shoe was wedged against a hot-water pipe by the wall, and the other was almost in the corridor.

"But what the Pakistanis did in your country's got a lot in common with what the Nazis did, and were going to do, in Poland. You know, they wanted Poland just as more space for Germans, and they wanted the Poles as work-animals, just work-animals. You know what they did? They went into villages and they rounded up all the leaders, all the organizers — the teachers, priests, mayors, doctors — all those kind of people — and they had them shot. In front of

71

their kids, wives, they just shot 'em. And there were standing orders that any Poles who took their places, became new leaders — they were going to be shot too. They thought if they killed anybody who showed any intelligence, any organizing ability, then eventually they'd turn the Poles into animals that they could use to do all Germany's dirty work. And they weren't going to let the Poles be educated, except they'd teach them to count to fifty. That was all. No reading or writing, because they might get ideas from that . . . And the Nazis said it was okay to do that to the Poles because they were only Slavs anyway, and Slavs were an inferior race — degenerate. Like the Jews . . . And *they* don't know *any* of this!" He indicated the rest of the school with a sudden, wide swing of his arm. His hand banged into the wire grid behind him, and it clanged and hummed.

"A lot of them know exactly what the Nazis did," Kamla said. "They want to do the same."

"I know. Somebody ought to tell the kids with 'British Movement' tattooed on their hands that the Nazis didn't only kill Germans who were Jews — they killed Germans who were Jehovah's Witnesses too, and Germans who were Trade Unionists, and Germans who listened to the BBC! And Russians and Poles. Who would they have killed when all the Jews and Slavs, and everybody who disagreed with them, was dead? That's what these kids should think about. They'd still want somebody to blame for whatever was going wrong. People with red hair, would it be, instead of people with a different language or colour skin? Or all people over six feet tall, maybe."

"They wouldn't listen to you, or believe you, whatever you said," Kamla told him.

"No. People believe what they want to believe. Some of the morons say the whole business of the Final Solution is Jewish lies to discredit the Nazis. Can you *credit* — ?"

"Such stupidity," she finished for him.

"Have you seen those films of the dead Jews being shovelled into graves with bulldozers? Do you know, they say the bodies aren't Jews, they're allied airmen's bodies, and the bodies of people killed in air-raids? They say the Jews collected together all these bodies and then made the film to show the Nazis in a bad light . . . They say that, and they *believe* it, and there are these bodies, so thin, all their bones sticking out, skeletons — and no burns, no broken bones, no injuries — some air-raid victims! How can people make themselves believe such shit?" He looked at her, eyes wide. She shook her head. Then he surprised her by smiling. "It takes a shit to believe shit!" The smile quickly vanished and his face quivered, for an instant, into an expression that suggested he was close to tears before returning to its usual blankness. Kamla sat up a little straighter, realizing suddenly that what he was saying mattered to him far more deeply than she had supposed. "Those people were gassed — or shot in the back of the head — and then they cut off their hair to use in precision instruments. They farmed them. They turned their fat into soap —"

"They *what*?" Kamla had actually jumped with shock at this grisly remark. She was sure she had misheard.

He lifted his eyes and looked at her. "They rendered down the bodies — in some camps — and turned the fat into soap." Kamla sat back, her face horrified. "The Jews used to have a joke. When people were taken away to be killed, their friends would say, 'Never mind, we'll meet again — when we're both bars of soap in a shop-window.' And they had to say, 'No, we won't — because I'll be expensive toilet soap, and you'll be cheap laundry soap.' "

For a while Kamla sat rigidly, her face twisted with disgust. Then she relaxed and said, "Oh, I don't believe that!"

"It's true."

"It can't be. Who would wash with soap that —"

73

"They built huge camps, just to kill people in," Jonathan said. "They burned the bodies in specially built incinerators, and there are twelve feet of human ashes in the fields round Auschwitz. They pulled the teeth out of the corpses' mouths to get the gold. They killed everyone who couldn't work as soon as they reached the camps — the old people, the children, the pregnant women. They did all that, and you don't believe they turned human fat into soap? Waste not, want not, you know."

"Oh, the Jews, the Jews!" Kamla said suddenly. "It's just as if the Jews are the only people in the world who ever suffered anything — European, white Jews! It doesn't matter about the Palestinian refugees, dying in their camps — it doesn't matter about the Lebanese people being bombed and strafed by Israeli planes, does it?"

Jonathan was doubled over his legs, his big hands holding his head. Still doubled over, he turned his head to look at her. "Was it okay, then, to kill six million — ?"

"I don't think the Jews should be the only ones to be remembered! You were the one talking about all the people killed since 1900. What about the people killed in Argentina, Chile, Uganda, Cambodia? I read in a newspaper that the Japanese had terrible torture camps where they kept Chinese and American prisoners, and they froze them, and broke their bones and gave them gangrene — all kinds of horrible experiments — And I read," she rushed on, as she saw him about to speak, "that when the Americans won the war, they let the people who ran the camps and did the experiments go free in exchange for all the records of the experiments! And they used what they learned from the experiments in Korea and Vietnam! The wonderful Americans! So why is it always the German Nazis and the Jews?"

Jonathan slumped, silent. "That's just the point," he said. "There's nothing unusual about Nazis. They're everywhere . . ." Almost apologetically, he added, "I just think it's important it should be *remembered*."

Most of Kamla's anger died at last. It seemed that she had won anyway, Jonathan seemed so sad. He gave her nothing to argue against.

They sat on either side of the cloakroom in silence — from which they were startled by the opening of a classroom door a little further along the corridor. Through it, angrily, came Miss Bight. Seeing them she stopped, one hand still on the handle of the door. "Is it you two who have been doing all that shouting?" She came into the middle of the corridor, putting her hands on her hips. "What are you doing here? Don't you have a lesson?"

Kamla stood. "No, Miss Bight. Not this lesson. I'm sorry. We — "

"Are you in the sixth form?" The teacher looked at Kamla's trousers and then at her face again. Kamla nodded. "Then shouldn't you be in the library, studying? Isn't that what you've stayed on for?"

"Yes, Miss, but —"

Miss Bight moved her head impatiently. "Should you or shouldn't you?"

"Yes, Miss." There was an intensity of disapproval in the teacher's face which, Kamla guessed, wouldn't have been there had she been talking to a white girl. It was an expression of: how dare you be brown-skinned and do this too? The disapproval became even more marked when the teacher looked at Jonathan; and curiosity became mingled with it.

"Then you'd better go there, quickly," Miss Bight said. As Kamla picked up her briefcase the teacher added, in a lower, half-enquiring voice, "I thought you weren't supposed to associate with young men. What would your parents say?"

Kamla's whole body leapt with anger; her fist clenched on the handle of her bag, the muscles of her arm jumped. She glared at the teacher as she passed her, and Miss Bight stared back, infuriatingly smug and unhurtable. Walking

75

up the corridor, knowing that the teacher was watching her, Kamla felt her feet stumble clumsily as the muscles of her legs quivered; she felt sick with anger. Behind her, she heard the teacher say, "Not *you*" — and a moment later, Jonathan caught up with her. Miss Bight didn't try to give him any more orders. They heard her classroom door close behind her.

"Oh, that *woman*!" Kamla said furiously. Tears rushed into her eyes as she spoke. Bight reminded her of the other woman, the one on the bus. They turned a corner in the corridor and came to more cloakrooms. Kamla turned aside into one and threw herself down on the narrow bench. She turned her head aside, her mouth tightly closed, her mind just as tightly closed with anger. She could think of nothing; only feel.

Jonathan stood and shuffled in the entrance of the cloakroom, as if waiting for her to get up and go on again. "This lesson's nearly over," he said. When she didn't move, he sat opposite her again, and studied her, then reached out a hand. But when she looked up at him, he didn't touch her, but turned his hand over, palm upward, above her knee. The wrist and hand were incongruously thin and delicate and its movement somehow sympathetic, and graceful. "Hey," he said. "You shouldn't give a shit for a shit like her."

Kamla grimaced with exasperation. She wished he wouldn't use that word. Did he think it clever?

As soon as Kamla could get away from her last lesson before lunchtime, she stuffed all her books into her bag, half-ran from the building and crossed the yard to the Art-wing. She wanted to catch Jonathan before he went somewhere else. She stopped in the yard outside the window of Mr. Kahn's room and looked in, but she couldn't see Jonathan. He might be in the Pottery-room on the other side of the building. She went into the Art-wing by a side door.

There was a small crowd just inside the Pottery-room, looking up at the wall behind the door. Kamla looked too, and saw stripes of bright red and white, so large that it took her a second or two to resolve them into a painting of a fluttering flag. At first glance, it appeared to be a painting of the Stars and Stripes, but there was something wrong about the dark-blue corner where the stars should have been painted, and she looked again. There was only one star; it was poised above a crossed hammer and sickle, also painted in white on the dark-blue ground. Around the flag words were daubed in thick, black paint, the lettering so bad that they were hard to read. She tried to make out what they said while the younger children teased Jonathan, trying to make him lose his temper. His painting was good, but what was it? How much would he want to paint their kitchen? Was his name Leonardo? And so on and so on. Jonathan ignored them all. Kamla eventually managed to make out the word scrawled above the flag — "Afghan-istan". All round the flag were the names of wars — Vietnam, Lebanon, Bangladesh — and the names of other countries, such as Poland, Czechoslovakia, Chile. If he expected them and the flag to mean anything to the people at Edward Brownheath, Kamla thought, he was going to be disappointed. She was glad when a teacher came in and ordered all the little so-and-sos out. He gave her a long look too, but guessed that she was a member of the sixth form, and followed the younger children out into the corridor without speaking to her.

She went over to where Jonathan was standing with one foot on a chair, and one foot on the wall cupboard, and rapped her knuckles on the cupboard top rather than say his name. When he looked down and saw her, he stepped clumsily and heavily down. "I was going to come and look for you after," he said.

She put her hands in her jacket pockets, holding her head well up. "I've got a great idea. You know you wanted the

77

people in this school told about the Nazis? Well, listen. In the Resource Centre, there's a new photostat machine. It makes really good copies — I know, because I've helped with the school magazine. In five minutes you can make two hundred copies." Jonathan sat down on the edge of a table, his head tilted to one side. "Now, I'm a sixth-former, and I've got this reputation as a really good girl — always do my work, write neatly, all that. So I can get away with murder. Nobody would mind me using the machine, and even if they asked what I was doing, I could say I was running something off for a lesson, and they'd believe *me*. I could photostat anything."

Jonathan nodded, rocking himself backwards and forwards on the edge of the table, and grinning. "That," he said, "is a fantastic idea."

6

At lunch-time the following day, Kamla went down to the first sitting and ate quickly. Instead of returning to the library she climbed the stairs to room 43, where she had arranged to meet Jonathan, away from the curiosity of pupils and teachers.

He was already there, sprawled on one of the little chairs, his legs spread wide and heavy in the aisle. He smiled as she closed the door behind her. Kamla didn't smile. She was concerned to keep things business-like. She didn't want to give him any excuse for misunderstanding her reasons for meeting him alone in a classroom so far from everyone else.

She marched down the aisle, stopping at the desk behind him and setting her briefcase on it. She took out the large brown envelope in which she had tidly packed all the things she intended to reproduce in their bulletin. She would have liked to write something original for it, but there wasn't time. She wanted to produce it immediately, before she thought too much about it and decided that she had better not go through with it. So she had cut several articles from magazines and newspapers: one about the Nationality Act, which explained the three grades of British citizenship that had been introduced, and the implications for people who lost their citizenship because of it; another about the apartheid laws of South Africa and the money from British investors which helped to support the apartheid system; an article discussing the racially biased reporting of the riots in Brixton, Birmingham and Liverpool, which had reinforced the white notion that blacks were troublemakers; several cuttings about racialist attacks on black or Asian people where the police seemed reluctant to admit that the attacks *were* racialist, or to take enquiries for the attackers very far: an interview with a Sikh police cadet, who told of the extreme racism he had encountered among his fellow cadets; and an interview with some Asian boys who had been arrested after violent incidents provoked by a National Front march through their home streets. The march had been against police advice, and the boys claimed that members of the National Front had also been violent, yet no member of the NF had been arrested.

Another cutting told of an experiment carried out by a newspaper, which arranged interviews for jobs with a large corporation for two young men who had actually been journalists. One man was black, one white. Both had equal qualifications for the job, and both were well-groomed and well-spoken. The white reporter had been treated with friendliness, and though he had not been offered that particular job, had been invited to apply to the firm again, in a slightly different capacity, and his name had been added to a waiting list. The black reporter had been met with polite discouragement and told that he was not suitable for the position. When he asked why not, he was told that things were moving fast in industry and his qualifications were not quite what the firm was looking for.

Jonathan got up from his chair and, sitting on the desk beside her briefcase, looked through the articles as she took them from the envelope and passed them to him. "Great," he said, which annoyed her. She knew he meant that the articles she had chosen would make their point well in the bulletin, but it still sounded callous.

"What have you found?" she asked, half-expecting to discover that he hadn't bothered to find out anything at all. That was usually the way things went. But, still reading one of her articles, he took a creased and folded bundle of papers from his jeans pocket and passed them to her. She opened them out. Of course, they were all about the German Nazis and the Final Solution. It was entirely reasonable of her to be concerned about racism in Britain — it was happening now, and she was frequently a victim of it — but she thought that there was something odd about Jonathan's obsession with events of forty years ago.

Most of Jonathan's contribution had been copied from books. She was shocked by his handwriting. Her little brother, who was only nine, wrote better. How had he gone through school, and reached his age, without learning to write more respectably than this ugly, difficult scrawl? It would all have to be typed out before it could be read. There was a typewriter in the Resource Centre, but she doubted whether Jonathan could type, and sighed. She would end up doing it.

She puzzled over his writing and made out something about a riot, called the Crystal Night Pogrom, in 1938. It had been ordered and organized by the Nazi Government, and in many towns had been led by Professors and their students. The mobs had burnt synagogues, destroyed Jewish shops, and attacked Jewish homes. Hundreds of Jewish people were killed or injured, twenty-six Jewish men were sent to concentration camps, and twenty thousand others were imprisoned. Then the Nazis made the Jews pay for all the damage the riots had caused.

There was much, too, about the way the Nazis had steadily taken all rights from the Jews. They had begun by taking away their citizenship: Jews were declared to be no longer German, no matter how long they and their families had lived in Germany, worked for Germany, paid taxes for Germany. After their citizenship had been denied, and they had been made aliens, then it was so much easier to prevent

81

Jewish children receiving any education, to prevent Jews from using any public place, to forbid Jewish doctors, lawyers, teachers and other professionals to practise their professions. Reading it, Kamla nodded. She saw how she could print this article and the one about the Nationality Act, together, perhaps even side by side. They complemented each other. Wasn't the citizenship of many black Britons being questioned?

"Oh — there's this too." Jonathan leaned over to the desk where he had been sitting and picked up a paperback book. She glimpsed the Nazi swastika in its red circle before he opened the book and folded it back to show her two photographs, printed one above the other.

She took the book, and studied them. Nothing he had told her gave her a deeper and more lasting sympathy for the Jews the Nazis had murdered than those photographs. The top one showed a man, a Jew, being made to walk down a street by armed Nazi guards. His shoes and trousers had been taken from him; he walked barefoot, in his long-johns and coat. A sign had been hung round his neck; the caption beneath the picture translated it — "I am a Jew, but I have no complaints about the Nazis". The photo was old and dark, and not much could be told from the man's face, though he seemed quite calm. He was holding his head up, despite what they were doing to him. Kamla admired him for that. She did not need to be told of the helpless rage he was enduring: rage that was controlled, but not eased, by fear for himself and his friends and family. She did not need to be told how, afterwards, he must have heaped pointless rebukes upon himself for not resisting this humiliation — how could he have resisted? Poor, poor man — and no one among the guards, or in the watching crowd, was giving him any sign of sympathy or friendship — no more than the people on the bus had given her when that woman had humiliated her.

The picture below was, in a way, even worse. It showed

people arriving at Auschwitz, the death-camp. A long queue of men with stars sewn on their coats were being inspected by a German soldier, who was, the caption said, choosing which of them were to be gassed to death immediately, and which of them were to be "exterminated through work".

From her brown paper envelope Kamla took a photograph she had cut from a local Asian magazine, and passed it back to Jonathan with his book. It showed an Asian groceries shop. The plate-glass windows had been smashed, and the glass in the door, and a swastika had been scrawled on its wall and on the pavement in front of it. "Great!" Jonathan said again, when he saw it.

"No, it's *not* great!" she snapped. He looked at her a moment, but said nothing. Instead he opened his book to another section of photographs, and passed it back to her.

A man in striped pyjamas slumped weakly among a heap of rags and bodies, eyes staring through the camera from a face no thinner than the faces she had seen in a hundred Oxfam advertisements, but with a deep and startling lack of hope, staring through forty years, at her. And there was a photograph of a pit jammed full of bodies, skin-covered skeletons.

There were photographs as horrific taken in all modern wars: Vietnam, Cambodia, Biafra, Bangladesh . . . But the thought was anything but comforting. That was why the man in the striped pyjamas had been photographed. Ask him if there was any hope of a Third World War (possibly nuclear) being avoided. Trying to comprehend the number of people whose lives, thoughts, ideas, worlds, had been ended, with as little consideration and feeling as she would bring to the throwing away of a piece of scrap paper, she suddenly said, "How could they *do* this? How could they bear to do it? What kind of people — ?"

Jonathan, flipping through her collection of clippings, said, "Children."

"Children?" Children were cruel, yes, but even so . . . She looked at him, thinking that he had spoken flippantly, for effect. He raised his eyes to her face quite seriously. He had simply given her what he felt to be the answer to her question.

"Children, yeah. Adult bodies, but children in their minds. Look at the excuses they made — 'I was only obeying orders.' 'I had to do as I was told.' 'It was unpleasant, but it was necessary for Germany's good. It had to be done.' They thought they were being really manly and tough — 'A tough man's got to do what only a tough man can do.' Only children think like that . . . They force themselves to do it, and they think they're proving something — but when they're caught out — 'Oh, it wasn't my fault, I didn't mean it really, it was orders, it had to be done . . .' And if you ask me, all leaders, everywhere, are like that."

Having eaten their dinners, the Resistance Movement of the Edward Brownheath School gathered in the yard: Sharon, Joanne, Anita, Carol and Diane. They stood close together, and hinted at what they were going to do, made vague threats and giggled, and finally linked arms in a chain and wandered about the yard, looking for someone to resist. It was hard. There were some tall West Indian boys kicking a ball about, and the girls looked at each other and tittered, agreeing without words that the boys were far too big and energetic for them to attack. A much smaller black boy passed them a few minutes later, and they looked at him hard, consideringly, and then stopped and turned towards each other, sniggering again. The boy didn't even notice them.

"Well, he's a *boy*. . . ." Carol said, through her giggles, meaning that, although shorter than they, he was intimidatingly thick-set and strong-looking.

"Anyway . . ." Anita said, which meant that, anyway, he

hadn't done anything to them. Mary Ullman had offended one of their friends, so it was easy to get angry about her. When someone hadn't done anything at all, it was hard to attack them.

Girls seemed an easier proposition, but even though they marched round the yard, looking for a black girl to attack, there was always something to put them off. If they found a girl on her own, then she was too big, or too sparky-looking, likely to fight back. Mostly there were two or three girls together, and they couldn't be sure that they could beat all of them. Even though they were continually telling each other that *next* time, no matter what, they would have a go, somehow, when they came upon another black girl, or group of black girls, they found themselves giggling, exchanging looks and sliding by, without so much as shouting 'boo!'

Sharon was growing more and more annoyed. They *had* to break out of this tittering cowardice; they just had to force themselves, it had to be done. This wasn't the way the Resistance had behaved. As all five of them swung round to go back across the yard yet again, Sharon saw a party of Indian girls sitting on a wall. This was it, she thought; they were the ones. Indian girls were meek and mim; they were quiet and polite and didn't fight. Dragging on the arms of Joanne and Anita, she made towards them, and the other four jostled and stumbled with her. "Gabble, gabble," Sharon yelled, because the Indian girls were not talking in English. "Can't you talk English?"

The others caught the idea. Joanne squealed, "Why don't you go back where they talk gabble-gabble?"

"Wogs!" Diane said.

The Indian girls looked up and round, surprised but contemptuous. They were all older than Sharon and her friends. They raised their brows, laughed together at the white girls, and continued with their talk.

The Resistance Movement continued to heckle them.

85

"Wog, wog, woggies!" Joanne yelled, and looked at her friends, giggling wildly, hoping for their approval.

Carol shouted and asked if the colour came off; Anita remarked on the smell in that part of the yard. They were delighted to see that their taunts were irritating one of the Indian girls; she kept looking over her shoulder with a scowl. She had a thin, gypsyish face, and her long, black hair hung loose over her arms and back. They began to address their remarks to her, laughing out loud and skipping with excitement. The thin girl finally had enough. She rose from the wall almost at a run, and came at them with an angry and threatening face, her hand raised to slap, her hair flying. It was Parvinder.

Even though there were five of them, and only Parvinder threatened them, the white girls unlinked their arms and ran in all directions. All the time they had been shouting and gibing they had been on edge, half-knowing that they were wrong, and fearing retaliation. When it came, they hadn't the nerve to stand and meet it. Only Sharon, as she ran, realized that, as a member of a Resistance group, she shouldn't be running; she should be fighting. She stopped, and turned, as she thought, at bay; turned right into Parvinder's arms, and Parvinder, without any of Sharon's heroic airs, took hold of her by the arm, as her mother might, and slapped her once, hard, across the ear, crying, "You have *that*!" Sharon shook with shock and fright, still in Parvinder's grip. Her mouth dropped open; her head vibrated and rang with the blow; she was quite unnerved and unable to do anything to defend herself.

"Calling me and my friends names!" Parvinder said, in the manner of Sharon's mother, as she stood over her angrily. "Who do you think you are, Madam?" And she shook Sharon by the arm. Sharon was dwarfed, frightened, embarrassed by the knowledge that she had been cheeky to this tall, angry, motherly, adult girl who was, even Sharon recognized, perfectly justified in her anger. The other

Indian girls came up behind Parvinder, and Sharon looked down at her feet, blushing bright red. She felt such a fool. Where was all her toughness, her patriotic resistance, now?

Parvinder lowered her own head close to Sharon's. "You silly, nasty little girl, calling your elders names like that. Do you want me to smack your bottom like a baby?" Sharon didn't answer, didn't look up, only shivered with fright and shame. She felt close to tears. Parvinder shook her again, and then pushed her away. "Go away, silly baby!" The other Indian girls put their arms across Parvinder's shoulders, and laughed with her, and they all went back to their seats on the wall. Sharon raised her head. Parvinder blew her a kiss, which made them all clap their hands and laugh the louder. Tears in her eyes, Sharon ran away across the yard. A few minutes before, she had been like Natalie: tall, slim, strong, capable, tough, striding across the yard with masculine grace and a sub-machine gun. Now she felt physically shorter; she felt her chubbiness and clumsiness; she felt how much of a child she was. And she realized that Parvinder had never seen her as anything else.

As she ran across the yard, she met Joanne, Carol, Anita and Diane, with simpering, uncertain faces. They had seen her slapped by Parvinder, from a distance, and they thought it funny, but they knew that Sharon didn't, and they wanted to appear sympathetic. Sharon stopped, and let them come up to her. "Where were you?" she shouted. "You all ran off fast enough, didn't you? Oh *yes*!"

They shrugged their shoulders, gathering nervously round her. "What are we going to do now?" Diane asked.

Sharon knew that Diane was hoping they would all agree to forget the idea of the Resistance Movement; Diane had been half-hearted about it all along. "We can't give up," Sharon said fiercely. "The Resistance had a lot of failures — *they* never gave up. So we can't." Already she felt the strength of the Resistance coming over her. Grit your teeth and force yourself to go on, no matter what. Sometimes it was unpleasant, sometimes you felt that you might be behaving wrongly, but you just had to ignore all that and concentrate on what had to be done, on what was necessary.

So, with linked arms, they began to roam round the yard again. They passed a black boy, standing by himself, looking round for his friends, and the other four all looked at Sharon. Her blush returned, but she didn't call the boy names. She led them all past him. The others began to titter. It was a ridiculous failure, this Resistance idea, and it had been Sharon's idea. Then Sharon saw Mary Ullman come round the corner of the school building, into the open yard. There was no reason to hold back from Mary. She was alone; and they already knew that she didn't fight back. Sharon unlinked her arms from Joanne's and Carol's, and ran forward, yelling, "Mary! Gonna get you — look out!" Behind her, her four soldiers charged, yelling, "Hurray!"

Mary looked startled and scared. She turned and ran a little way, and then stopped. She turned round and stood waiting for them. They rushed up to her and round her, bumping into her, surrounding her — and there was an uneasy pause as they wondered what to do next. Sharon, already furious, and viciously ready to hurt someone, solved the problem by pounding Mary on the back with her clenched fist, to a chant of, "I didn't do it hard enough yesterday!"

"Go on — give her some more, Shaz!" Joanne said.

"I'll give her some more!" Mary was retreating, and Sharon dragged her back by her cardigan. "Jew!" She kicked Mary on the shin.

Energized by fear and rage, her face swollen, wet and scarlet, Mary began to slap and push at Sharon. Through tears, she shouted, "*Don't* say that! I'm not a Jew."

They laughed at her. "So *you* say!" Carol said.

"We know you're a Jew," Joanne said.

Nervous about the noise Mary was making, noise that might attract a teacher's attention, Sharon said, "Cry-baby

— blart-a-lot! Shut up!" She slapped Mary's head as Parvinder had slapped hers, and felt revenged.

She had raised her foot to kick Mary again when she saw, over the shoulders of the others, Parvinder, followed by her friends. Parvinder made her way into the circle round Mary by dragging Joanne out of it backwards, and then shoving Carol away so hard that she almost fell down. As Sharon lowered her foot to the ground and took a wary step backwards, Parvinder pulled Mary towards herself, and pushed her backwards into the arms of Nerinder and Padma. "So, you start on someone else now!" Parvinder said, hands on her hips.

Carol, Anita, Joanne and Diane were edging away, their eyes wide. They were all annoyed that Parvinder should interfere like this. It wasn't as if they had been on to an Indian girl. "Why don't you mind your own business — Blackie!" Sharon yelled, her face ugly with anger, and taking on a purple tint.

"You had to go and find someone on her own, I know!" Parvinder said, still slowly and calmly coming at Sharon. Sharon backed away. "Coward!" Parvinder said. "Get out of here before I give you that smacked bottom!"

"None of your business!" Almost crying again, Sharon spat and spluttered. "You big, black —"

Parvinder stopped strolling and ran at her. Sharon turned round and raced away, and Parvinder stood still and laughed. "Coward!" she shouted again, and then turned, her long hair flying in the air, and went back to her friends.

Nerinder had her arms round Mary, holding her and making shush, shush noises. Padma stood by her, trying to see Mary's face. Parvinder took Mary from Nerinder and said, "Hush-up now; there; you come and stay with us. They'll be scared to come after you then."

"You come and find us every break now," Nerinder said, looking at Parvinder for confirmation. "We won't let them hurt you."

89

Mary looked round at them, wiping her face with her fingers. They stared back at her, with kindness and curiosity, until she became shy and looked down at the concrete. She muttered, "Thanks," under her breath.

"Come on then." Parvinder led the way back to the wall where Shobana and Raj were waiting. Shy, and rather bewildered, Mary was seated among them. Parvinder told her all their names, and Mary gave them each a sharp, brief glance, before looking at the ground again. Nerinder offered her some sweets from a crumpled white bag, and Mary hesitated — but they were only humbugs, such as any white girl might have. She took one and sat holding it in her hand, unwilling to eat it. Parvinder began telling her how Sharon and her gang had been calling them names before they had started on her, and so she, Parvinder, had decided to sort them out. Mary was only half-listening. She wondered if people from her class were looking at her, sitting there with them, and thinking her a Paki-lover. It was funny, really, that they should ask her to sit with them, because she didn't like Indians. She thought they were stuck-up. But she stayed with them because, with them, she was safe from Sharon's gang.

In room 43 Jonathan and Kamla had spread the clippings over two desks, trying to decide how the bulletin would be arranged. "There's another thing I want to do, too," Kamla said. "I want to draw up a list of — well, of racists — and print that."

"How do you mean?" he said.

"People like Cherie Reed. She's *so* pretty, but her nature's not. And all the teachers who absolutely ignore me and only help the white kids. The ones who said I wasn't good enough to do O-level English "

"Said *you* weren't?"

"I passed English Literature and Language, but Miss

Hammond said I didn't have the flair — my Dad had to make a fuss before they would let me do it. I'd like to put all their names in the bulletin." She looked down at the clippings, waiting for his reply, and none came. "I suppose you don't like that?"

"No, it's not that. The best thing you can do with a Nazi is to expose them for what they are."

"I didn't say they were Nazis!" Him and the pestilential Nazis.

"All racists are Nazis . . . They're everywhere . . . No, what I was worried about was that it'll get you into a lot of trouble . . ."

She nodded. It certainly would. She had been trying not to think about the trouble.

"I mean," he went on, "they might even let us do something like this if we asked — censored and approved, watered-down and prettied-up — but they might let us do it. But they'd never let us print a list of guilty names, especially not if it includes teachers' names."

Kamla felt her stomach roll with fear as she realized just what an uproar it would cause. Teachers would be against her; children would be against her; she might even be expelled. Her parents would be furious; they wouldn't see her side of it, they wouldn't sympathize with why she had done it at all. They would be shocked. And, if she was expelled, what about her studies? How would she get the qualifications for Medical School then? But despite all this, despite all the distress and misery she quite plainly saw ahead of her, she remained determined to go on with the bulletin and the list of names. If every protester gave up in the face of such threats, no one would ever protest . . . If she were expelled, there were other schools, there were night-schools. She was clever, she worked hard. She would get to Medical School anyway. So she was going to do it.

"When they find out about this," Jonathan said, "they're going to come straight to me. I could say it was all my idea."

"Oh, and get my credit too!" Kamla said. Who did he think he was, being so condescending, so kind? "I shall put my name on it. I'm *proud* of it. I *want* people to know who's responsible."

He grinned. "Okay! Great! Put my name on it too." Straightening, he tipped back his head and waved his fist at the ceiling in a noble revolutionary pose. "We'll defy them all!"

Kamla gathered up all the clippings and replaced them in her brown envelope. She watched him with amusement from the corners of her eyes. "Stupid," she said.

At a quarter to four, having had a cup of coffee in the staffroom, Mags Firth went along to the Resources Centre. She wanted to look through the posters and tapes in hope of finding some inspiration for a lesson the following week. Through the glass door of the Centre she saw Jonathan Ullman and Kamla Momen. Jonathan was at the photo-stat machine, and Kamla was expertly using the typewriter, rattling away at a speed Mags envied. Jonathan saw her and watched her with his usual suspicious surliness as she went into the room, but Kamla was absorbed in her typing and jumped when Mags called out, "Hello, you two!"

Jonathan just glowered. Kamla, putting her hand to her chest, turned in her chair, smiled, and said, "Hello, Miss Firth," as politely and charmingly as ever. Mags smiled. She liked Kamla, remembering her from earlier years. She was not only polite and well-behaved, but intelligent and eager to learn. You could always rely on Kamla to give whatever work was set a slant of her own, which, with forty pieces of work to mark from most classes, was a precious thing. "What are you doing? Anything interesting?" Mags asked.

"Oh, I'm just preparing something for a lesson," Kamla said, looking at her with another smile. "Jonathan said he would help me — " Seeing Mags look in some surprise at the photo-stat machine churning out so many copies, Kamla added, "It's a project — a questionnaire — it's for Economics, you know. I have to find out how everyone in the school feels about ice-creams, its colours and flavours and so on — and make up statistics from it."

"Hmm," Mags said, thinking that someone was doing some enterprising teaching. "Is it part of your A-level course?"

Kamla turned her head towards Jonathan for a second, then looked at Mags again. "No. It's just to help us understand statistics better, and how they can be twisted."

"Sounds more like Maths to me," Mags said.

"Oh, it all comes into Economics, Miss."

Mags grimaced again, to show how impressed she was. "Well, I know nothing about Economics or Maths, thank God — I won't disturb you if I mess about in the background, will I? I don't quite know what I'm looking for."

"Oh no, Miss," Kamla said. "I'm going when I've finished this typing. I've got a bus to catch — Jonathan's going to finish here for me."

Jonathan glanced round at this mention of himself, and Mags gave him a big, warm smile. She thought that the friendship which was obviously growing between these two was rather cute. "Making yourself useful here as well as the Art-room, eh, Jonathan? I must say, it's very good of you to give our Kamla a hand."

He smiled slightly, and turned his attention to the machine again. Kamla turned back to the typewriter and began tapping the keys. Mags felt a little out of place. She strolled over to the posters, talking aloud to herself. "Now what would you say would make a really zappy lesson? Any bright ideas? Any fire-cracking inspirations . . .?" She saw them grinning at each other with suppressed, conspiratorial laughter, but she thought nothing of that. Half the kids in the school behaved in exactly the same way all the time . . .

And Jonathan Ullman was nothing but a big kid really. That was mostly why she liked him.

She soon became quite absorbed in pulling posters from their racks and studying them, and peering at the titles on cassettes. Nothing she thought up really appealed to her. She turned and called "Goodbye" when Kamla left and then became absorbed again, though she was aware that Jonathan was still behind her. She could hear him moving papers, and she heard him switch off the machine. Without its buzz the room, the whole school, was very quiet.

Presently she became bored. She wasn't getting any ideas; she was just becoming confused with possibilities. She decided to go home and sleep on it. Turning to leave, she saw Jonathan standing by the photo-stat machine, taking up papers and stapling them together with the big stapler he must have fetched from the main desk.

"Still here?" she said. He looked up, but made no answer to her obvious remark. She went over to him and sat on a table close by. He went on with his work of stapling together Kamla's questionnaire, but soon, casually, moved between her and the piles of paper. A moment later, he pushed them along the table, further from her. "When Kamla draws up a questionnaire, she really draws up a questionnaire," Mags said. He made no answer to that either, didn't even look at her. Mags wasn't offended. She wondered that people like Mr. Kendle couldn't see that what they called his surliness and rudeness was shyness. He didn't know how to chatter lightly. She thought that she would ask him a question he could answer — besides, she was curious to know the answer. "Do you speak German?"

He stopped stapling and looked at her. "No."

"Oh — I thought, with your parents being German —"

"My mother's German.

"Oh." Mags thought that over, and he shuffled the printed papers together, and did some more stapling. "You say Ullman isn't a German name? It sounds like one."

94

He shrugged. "My father's English."

"But I thought Mr. Kahn said —"

He stopped what he was doing again. "Kahna gets the wrong end of the stick. He's getting old. I told him my mother was German — so he takes it that I am. I told him about one of my mother's uncles who had a Jewish wife and so he got out before the War started. So Kahna gets it into his head that we're Jewish, like he is."

"Oh, I see," Mags said. She felt very let down. No chases across Europe after all. No glamorous suffering, no courage under persecution. "How did your mother and father meet, then, if she's German and —"

"He was in the army — he was in Germany."

"It's a funny coincidence — that she should marry an English soldier with a German name."

He shrugged. The stapling finished, he made a neat stack of the questionnaires. Then he stood and looked at Mags, as if he was considering whether or not to tell her something. She sat up straighter and tried to look worthy of confidences. He said, "She was in the Hitler Youth."

Mags blinked, not quite following. "Who was? Your *mother*?"

"Yeah. In the German Girls' League — the *Bund Deutscher Mädchen*. They took her on holiday, and they played games and sang — they'd sit round the fire and sing songs about winning the War for Hitler."

"Wow — that sounds wonderful!" Mags said, and laughed. She stopped laughing when he gave her a straight, annoyed look.

"It *was*," he said. "It *was* wonderful. My mother's family were poor, really poor. She spent all her free time doing her grandparents' farmwork for them, because her grandparents would have been kicked out of their little shack if she hadn't. They were too old, see. She'd never had a holiday. She never had any sweets or toys . . . Then the *Bund Deutscher Mädchen* took her on holiday. I tell you, she thought Hitler was *God*."

Good Lord, Mags thought, this is a long way from heroically escaping the S.S. in the dark of night. "Well . . . yes, I suppose — it must have seemed like that to people then," she said, politely, though inwardly she was certain that no one with any humanity, any decency, could have any admiration for Hitler at all.

"The Nazis made it better for her grandparents too, made it so they didn't have to work for their cottage. They did a lot of things like that, so she thought they were great . . . And when she was sixteen, she got engaged to a bloke in the S.S. There are photos of him at home."

Mags' mouth opened. She stared. "The S.S." He nodded seriously. This, she thought, is a bit rich. She studied him for signs that he was lying. His face was solemn and earnest.

"She would have married him, but he was sent to Russia, and he got killed. Right at the end of the War, that was. Her brother was killed too."

That was all that was needed, Mags thought, the decadent, leather-clad S.S. officer, romantically slain in the hell of the Russian front. She couldn't fit his honest, plain manner to the story he was telling. She seemed to remember seeing it in a dozen films.

"They did some terrible things in Russia . . . Do you think anybody like that can really change their minds, ever?"

Puzzling over why he should invent lies about his parents, she was taken off-guard by this question, and he repeated it. "Somebody who'd been in the Hitler Youth like that — been going to marry an S.S. — do you reckon they'd ever really change their mind?"

A question beyond her power to answer, if ever she'd heard one. "You mean about Hitler being God? . . . Who knows? Everything's possible."

He looked at her, then picked up the pile of question-naires. "Yeah," he said, and she thought his tone and expression contemptuous. "I suppose it is." Without wishing her goodnight, he crossed the room and went out into the entrance hall. She watched him go in some surprise, feeling snubbed and annoyed.

She remained sitting on the table, her arms folded, thinking over what he had told her. There must have been a lot of girls in the Hitler Youth; and a lot of people in the S.S. It wasn't inconceivable that two such people would become engaged. And a lot of people had been killed on the Russian front — that was why it had found its way into so many films and books. Maybe it wasn't such a wild story . . . But why did the story of Jonathan's family escaping from the Nazis seem so much more believable? She felt herself pulled that way . . . To claim to be the son of a Hitler-worshipper seemed so melodramatic to her. By comparison, claiming to be from a Jewish refugee family seemed cosy, small and nice: well within the bounds of what was likely. She thought of crowded kitchens in London's East End, lively talk, hugs and jokes and chicken-soup . . .

But why would Jonathan lie? And then she remembered the way he had insisted that his father was English, despite his name — and the name, Ullman, was not only foreign, it was Jewish, surely. It wasn't the first time she had received the impression that he was ashamed of being Jewish — but he surely wasn't an admirer of Hitler. Was he? She tried to remember exactly what he had said, and couldn't be certain. Why tell such an elaborate story of S.S. officers and German maidens if it wasn't true?

Unless he had been trying to see how big a story he could get her to swallow. She had certainly sensed some hostility from him, for some reason, and his face and manner had been suspiciously deadpan throughout the telling . . .

She slipped off the table and picked up her bag, wishing there were some way of letting him know that she hadn't believed a word of his Nazi romance, not for a moment . . .

7

Jonathan came to school the next morning carrying the photo-copied bulletins under his arm. As he walked through the street, he chose houses at random, went up the paths, and posted bulletins through their doors.

Wandering through the school, he dropped some of them in a cloakroom, in the shadow of the coats; went into a boys' lavatory and left some on the windowsill; dropped some on the floor of the girls' lavatory. He stepped through a side door and left some in the corner of the porch, and went up to the library, where a teacher was working with a class. Jonathan opened the library door so quietly that only a few of the class noticed him, and tucked some of the bulletins into a rack of paperbacks. Others he put on the tables in the coffee-bar, some on padded seats in the entrance hall, many on radiators all over the school.

He went into the Art-room. Mr. Kahn was teaching, and Jonathan sat on the edge of the teacher's desk. Once he had set the children drawing, Mr. Kahn came over to him. From the desk he picked up a copy of the bulletin and held it out.

"You've found one already," Jonathan said.

"Then you are responsible for this." Mr. Kahn pinched the cigarette from his mouth between his fingers and thumb.

"It's got my name on it."

"Yes; and Kamla's. There's going to be a very unpleasant row about this."

"We know," Jonathan said.

"It's a very unpleasant thing," Mr. Kahn said, turning the bulletin over. "It makes it sound as if the only thing that exists in the world is — colour prejudice — and —" He shook the bulletin. "And people killing each other and smashing each other's windows —" Jonathan listened to him with a still face. "It does go on, you know," he said. "It does go on, you know," he said.

Mr. Kahn's face flushed. He scowled and shouted loudly, "I know it goes on, young man! I've seen more of it than you have!" The children in the class looked up, alarmed. They didn't laugh; they were all nervous of Mr. Kahn. Even Jonathan blinked. "But it isn't *all* that goes on," Mr. Kahn finished in a lower voice.

Jonathan was silent a moment, then said, "There wasn't room in a couple of pages for what Princess Di was wearing on her latest slumming trip, and photographs of kittens in champagne glasses."

There was no change in the expression either of his face or his voice, and there was a slight pause before Mr. Kahn fully understood him. Then Mr. Kahn's face turned redder still, and his voice rose again. "Now you're sneering! And you're sneering at *me*! And I won't have it, young man, because I'm right, you know! If there were only people like the people you write about, life wouldn't be worth living!"

Jonathan looked at him with pure disgust. "Oh — shit," he said. He rose from the desk, swinging away from Mr. Kahn towards the door, as if he couldn't bear to speak to him any more. "That's bullshit." He crashed the door back against the wall and ducked out of the room.

Mr. Kahn followed him, and shouted after him down the corridor. "What about Kamla? She could be expelled! Did either of you think of that?"

The Head's office was a large, square room, with tall

windows all along one wall. The smooth green carpet, the polished desk, the glass-fronted bookcase, all shone in the plentiful light. Mrs. Powell was reading the morning's letters at her desk when the telephone rang. She picked it up to hear her secretary telling her that a Mrs. Cullen, a parent, wanted to speak to her. Leaning back in her chair with a sigh, preparing herself, the Head gave the word for Mrs. Cullen to be put through.

Mrs. Cullen wanted to complain about the pamphlet that had been put through her door that morning. The Head didn't answer immediately; she didn't know why she should be held responsible for a pamphlet, but she wanted to find out what on earth Mrs. Cullen was talking about before committing herself. "I'm afraid I don't understand, Mrs. Cullen. Could you explain a little more, please?" Mrs. Cullen explained. A pamphlet headed 'Bulletin No. One' had been put through her door that morning, and it was quite obviously from the school because it said so at the end. It had a horrible picture of a starving man on the front, and pictures of dead bodies inside. Were these the kind of pictures they were showing Mrs. Cullen's children? Was this what was called education these days?

The Head still had no idea of what the woman was talking about. The school had issued no pamphlets, and certainly not pamphlets with horrible pictures. She was repeating that she didn't understand when another of the phones on her desk began to ring. She excused herself and answered the second phone, to be told by her secretary that a Mrs. Frank now wanted to speak to her — "About a bulletin and teachers being racist, or something like that."

As soon as she joined her English class, Kamla knew that Jonathan had distributed the bulletins. Normally there was a loud noise of chatter and laughter, even after the teacher came in, until they were called to order. Today there was silence as soon as she entered, and they all watched her as she made her way from the door to the desk at the back of the class where she always sat. There was a sense of waiting — for the moment when the teacher went away, perhaps — and this tension pervaded the whole lesson, even during their reading of the play. Kamla wondered what would happen when they were released. But what did you expect, she asked herself. That they would be pleased? She had printed nothing but the truth. Every name on that final list had been the name of someone she knew, from personal experience, to hold racist sympathies, and if they didn't like being called racists, then they should do some thinking. Whatever they did or said, she must remember that, and not allow them to intimidate her. She was proud of what she had done.

At the end of the lesson, while the teacher was still there, the other members of the class gathered their things and left the room. Kamla hung back, letting them get ahead. She had to decide where to spend the next fifteen minutes, the morning break. She could sneak down to the Art-rooms, where Jonathan would be, and spend the time with him; but what would everyone think of that? Besides, it was cowardly, running to his protection. It would be worse for her when he wasn't there. She could skulk about in the cloakrooms or lavatories but that would be cowardly too, and they would know that she was being cowardly. The only thing to do was to go to the library, as usual, and sit in her usual place; and then they would see that she wasn't ashamed of what she had done, but proud; and perhaps they would think that she wasn't afraid of the consequences either.

Nevertheless, she dawdled through the corridors. She passed side doors and saw, through the glass panes, the children who were locked out hitting each other with rolled up bulletins, making paper-planes out of them, kicking them about the yard and, in some cases, even reading them. In the entrance hall she saw a cluster of children standing round a copy of the bulletin that had been pinned to the notice-board, and another copy, the black and white picture of the starving man uppermost, lying on the floor half under one of the padded chairs outside the Head's office. She realized that copies must be spreading round the school; that if the staff didn't already know of them, they soon would do. What would happen? Would she only be shouted at, or would she be expelled? But she had done it to make a stir, and it seemed that she was succeeding. A small, flickering sense of excitement and pleasure rose in her, despite the cold qualms in her belly. Picturing in her mind all the people, throughout the school, with a copy of her bulletin in their hands, she thought: If you don't like what you're reading, then it serves you right!

When she pushed open the library door and went in, she found her fellow sixth-formers gathered round the central table, and more animated than usual. They had copies of the bulletin in their hands, and were reading them, or holding them up and declaiming, and laughing, jeering, talking. They looked round when Kamla entered, and a moaning, unpleasant sound began, a long-drawn-out 'oh'. More and more people joined in the sound as they looked round and saw Kamla too. She had stopped just inside the door, and stared back at them, trying to look more defiant than defensive, but not knowing if she was succeeding. "Oh, here she is," they said. "Here she is."

Kamla walked past the central table to the table in the corner where she usually sat. As she passed them, they began to cheer, on an unfriendly and scornful note. "Where's your boy-friend?" someone asked. "Hasn't he got nerve enough?" And someone else said childishly, "Can't he get his nose through the doors then?"

Pretending that she couldn't hear any of it, Kamla reached her table and sat with her back to everyone else, just as usual, though today she felt that she wanted to face them. It took a little extra courage to expose her back to them like that; she wasn't at all certain that they might not attack her. She took her books from her bag, kept her head up, and made a pretence of reading.

"I'd like — I'd like to know who they think they are!" said a shaky and tearful voice, which Kamla identified as Cherie's. Other voices rushed to sympathize, speaking more gently than before, to show what adult concern they could feel for poor, poor Cherie, whose name had appeared in the list of racists, and who had been terribly upset by it. "Yes," the voices said, "well they think they're better than everybody else, don't they? They sit in judgement —" Now that sounded *really* adult, and couldn't be given up — "They think they're court, judge and jury!"

Gloria, a black girl, was sitting in a chair under the window, reading a book and occasionally speaking to a friend who sat on the table beside her, but otherwise ignoring what was going on. A Sikh boy named Gopi got up and crossed the room, edging past people who blocked the aisles, and sat on the corner of Kamla's table. Voices from the central table called out, "Oh yeah, go on — stick together!"

"*You* stick together!" Gopi answered, and then smiled at Kamla, who had looked up at him questioningly. "I think that bulletin was great," he said, like Jonathan. Kamla nodded, smiling, quietly accepting the praise. With someone else's approval, it was so much easier to believe in the worth of what she had done herself.

The people at the central table kept talking, pretending to be talking among themselves, but always speaking loudly enough to be heard by Kamla and Gopi. "You've only got to *speak* and you're a racist these days! — Am I a racist? Have I ever been? — Well then! — What a nerve! — You can't win. If you're friendly to 'em, you're patronizing, and if you're not patronizing, you're a racist . . . Well, she's done *herself* no favours. Nobody'll want to talk to her after this!"

Gopi and Kamla smiled at what they heard. If these people weren't racist, how could they call Kamla 'cheeky', as they did, several times? Only inferiors can be cheeky. They didn't think of what they were saying, the people behind them. Gopi signalled to Barjhinder and Gupta, who had just come in. They came across and joined him and Kamla, and the cry went up again that they were "sticking together". Barjhinder and Gopi had seen the bulletin and read some of it, and they told Gupta, who had somehow missed it, all about it, in excited and approving terms. Gupta didn't seem impressed. He soon left them and sat by himself three tables away, reading. But the two other boys made amends for Gupta's depressing lack of appreciation. "How did you think of it?" Gopi asked. "I never would have, in a million years — and it's simple! Real genius!" Kamla smiled involuntarily, and felt herself glowing with what now seemed fully justified pride. She sternly told herself that she mustn't get carried away with this praise. She should prepare herself for when she was alone and exposed to the hatred of the white sixth-formers.

The bell rang to mark the end of break, and most of the people in the library rose. Kamla had to go to a Physics lesson. At the door she met Jane coming in. Jane stepped forward aggressively and, almost like the little skinhead thug Kamla had once met on the way into school, she said, "Don't get in my way, wog."

Cherie, giggling through her tears, said, "Oh, *Jane*!" in admiration at Jane's boldness in saying words that she would not dare to sully her own image with.

Never mind, Kamla thought; or at least, never mind so much. I've had my say about *you*; and you can't wipe it out.

"Take no notice," Gopi said.

Kamla answered, "But it just proves what I said, doesn't it?"

Gopi and Barjhinder accompanied her part of the way to the Physics lesson, and parted from her with much more friendly than usual goodbyes. But there was a lesson ahead of her in which she was the only Asian, and the only girl; and one where she didn't normally get on well with the other pupils. It was going to be no fun today. She felt queasy at the prospect, but she was determined not to give the slightest sign of being affected by whatever they said or did: not even if they hit her. She hoped she could live up to that. She reminded herself that, no matter what happened, it couldn't go on for ever; therefore she could survive it; and they were in the wrong and she was in the right.

She was glad to see, when she reached the open door of the Physics Lab, that Mr. Morley was already at his desk. She had dawdled so that he might reach the lesson first. She went in and carefully closed the door behind her. One of the boys at the second table leant over to another and whispered something; she heard them tittering. She walked between her table and theirs, watched by everyone, feeling hot and exposed. She had to turn her back on them, and clamber up on to the stool, which was awkward for her, since she was so small. They sniggered, and she felt herself growing angry. When she was finally seated on the stool, one of them made farting noises, and there was an outburst of fizzling laughter. She knew the noises and the laughter were aimed at her. "Oh, Kamla!" they whispered, in shocked voices. She looked steadily at Mr. Morley and the board, ignoring them. But they were seventeen, and more! What silly, silly, little boys.

Mr. Morley turned his back on the class and began wiping the board clean. One of the boys called out to him, "Better use the white-board, sir, if you don't want to be called a racist."

Mr. Morley half-turned and said, "What?" while the boys laughed out loud. He said irritably, "Oh, *shut up*, all of you," and concentrated on cleaning the board. Cheated of adult applause one of the boys whispered at Kamla's back, "Stuck-up Paki cunt."

"Paki" means pure, Kamla told herself; but it would be no good telling them. She couldn't get away from them until this double-lesson ended. Tears filled her eyes, but she set her face and wouldn't let them run. If she was sorry for herself, then she would begin wanting other people to be sorry for her, and pride didn't need pity.

Mr. Morley began the lesson, and she tried to concentrate on it and forget about the stupid children behind her; but her back was rigid and prickling with an awareness of their presence. The tightened muscles of her neck began to ache; her eyes were staring too wide and too fixedly at her book, and giving her a headache. She looked at her watch and saw that there was still an hour to go. An age later, there were still forty minutes left . . . And still three hours of the school day. She was so tense that she felt like screaming; there was so much nervousness and anger corked up inside her that she felt she might explode, especially when she heard the boys whispering again, calling her filthy names and making rude noises. Of course, she continued quietly with her work, though the thought came to her again and again that she *ought* to scream. She ought to petrify those stupid, silly boys with a heartfelt, full-throated scream. She *ought* to astonish them by throwing her bag at their heads. She ought to yell and rave and throw her stool through the windows. She ought to let them see how she felt, and startle and shock them into understanding.

But she didn't.

The lesson did, eventually, end. Because Mr. Morley was still at his desk, the boys collected their things and went out, talking noisily amongst themselves, but saying nothing to her. Only one of them, at the door, turned round and threatened her with his clenched fist. Except for height, there was not much difference between a sixth-former and a first-year. Kamla packed her belongings slowly into her bag, so that she wouldn't be following them too closely in the corridor. By chance, as she was doing this, she caught Mr. Morley's eye, and he suddenly gave her a smile, for no reason. Obviously, he hadn't yet seen a copy of the bulletin. She couldn't imagine that any teacher would smile at her like that after seeing it. Like everyone else, the teachers would stick together.

Mrs. Powell was sitting in her office with Mr. Kendle, looking through one of the many copies of the bulletin that had been handed to her, by sixth-formers and staff. She had skimmed through its collection of photographs and articles, and had carefully studied the list of racists' names at the end, rather relieved to find that her name was not among them. Following the list of racists were the words, "by Kamla Momen and Jonathan Ullman."

"Kamla Momen is that pretty Moslem girl in the sixth, isn't she? Who would have thought it of her? Of Jonathan, of course, it's no great surprise . . ."

Mr. Kendle did not say that if she distrusted him so much, she should never have allowed him into the school. He said, "It was photo-statted in Resources."

"Yes, I know, and how much do you think it cost?" Mrs. Powell peered closely at the paper and rubbed it with her thumb, as if valuing it.

"The paper is expensive . . . a pretty packet. It's possible that we could prosecute them for theft, you know, Mrs. Powell."

"Hmm," she said, thoughtfully. "Isn't Miss Firth in charge of Resources? I think I shall have a word with her before I send for Kamla or Jonathan . . . That really is a distressing picture they put on the front. No wonder our parents are upset . . ."

She didn't need to add any more. Mr. Kendle knew that parents who were upset could get in contact with newspapers and television and radio stations, and they would relay pictures and news of the school, not only to the general public, but also to the school governors and the education authorities. It was bad for the children, and it was very bad for the careers of senior staff, such as Heads and Deputy Heads.

"We must clear all this up, we really must," Mrs. Powell said. "Could you find Miss Firth for me, please, Mr. Kendle?"

The only part of the bulletin Sharon and Joanne read was the list of names at the end, which listed both Joanne's sister, Jane, and Jane's friend, Cherie, as racists. They pretended that it made them angry, but actually they were delighted, because the bulletin had been written by Jonathan Ullman, Mary's brother, and that gave them an excellent reason for getting Mary again. They'd never heard of Kamla Momen, and had no idea which of the thousand people at the school she was — or even if she was at the school.

They let Mary know of their intentions by leaning round other people and poking and punching her as they all stood in line for their meal at lunch-time. During the meal they were seated at different tables, but they kept signalling to Mary, waving their fists, grinning, and pointing to the yard. Mary looked sick and frightened, and that encouraged them.

They finished their meal before Mary, and waited for her outside the doors into the yard. A dinner-lady was posted near the door, to make sure that everyone went outside. They watched, their faces against the window, and they saw Mary go up to the dinner-lady, speak to her, and then go past her into the main body of the school. "Oh, she's said she wants to go to the toilet," Joanne said.

"Let's go in and say we do, then."

They went in. The dinner-lady watched them suspiciously as they crossed the entrance hall towards her, doubting them before they'd even told their story. They thought it unfair, even though they were going to lie to her. Joanne put her hand up, as if speaking to a teacher, and said, "Please, Miss, can we go and use the toilet?"

With a grim face, the dinner-lady nodded once. Looking at one another with joyful faces, Sharon and Joanne ran past her. The dinner-lady didn't tell them to stop running in the corridors. She knew her limitations.

They reached the first lavatory and went in. The sound of their footsteps became a thin echo, bouncing off the basins, tiles and pipes. There were five cubicles, four of them standing open, and one with its door closed. "Come out, come out, Mary," Sharon called, and looked at Joanne. They laughed together. "We know you're in here."

There was no answer. Putting a finger to her lips, Joanne crept into one of the open cubicles next to the closed one and, climbing on the lavatory seat, looked over the wall. In a second she jumped down, and waved to Sharon to go out into the corridor ahead of her. Laughing, gasping, they both pushed on the door and stumbled out, to lean on the corridor wall outside, giggling so much they couldn't speak.

"Was her — you know — on the pot?" Sharon managed, eventually.

Joanne couldn't answer immediately, but shook her head. "Hiding," she said, when she could. "Didn't see me."

"Well, quiet, quiet," Sharon said. "She'll hear us." But they went off into giggles again, both of them. "Quiet!" Sharon ordered sternly, when she had straightened her face. "We'll get her when she comes out, if you're quiet."

Not trusting herself to speak, in case she started laughing again, Sharon gave her further orders by signs. She waved Joanne back to an alcove in the corridor in front of the Medical room, while she herself went a little way up the corridor in the opposite direction, and hid in the cloak-rooms. They peeped out, saw each other, and had to clamp hands over their mouths to stop themselves laughing.

Neither of them was good at waiting patiently for long periods, but then excitement helped them to stick it out. Sharon whiled away time by thinking of the Resistance girl, Natalie, lying hidden in thick, long grass, her beret on her head, her sub-machine gun tucked close to her side, and a cigarette in her mouth. She thought that hiding in the cloakrooms, waiting for Mary to come out of the lavatory, must be something like what Natalie experienced as she lay waiting for German patrols — Mary was German too, so even that was the same! And if Natalie could wait for hours and hours like that, then she could wait a few minutes.

The lavatory door was pushed open a little way, and Sharon snatched her head back into hiding. A second later she carefully edged just enough of her head round the corner of the cloakroom for her to be able to see the lavatory door with one eye. Mary had poked her head out of the doorway and was taking a quick, timid look up and down the corridor. Sharon ducked out of sight again, just before she was seen, and the giggles, of excitement, and appreciation at her own cleverness, came bubbling up. She had to bite her lip to stop them.

Mary, thinking the corridor empty, gathered up the strap of her satchel and hung the bag from her shoulder. Sharon, peeping out, saw her actually pausing in the middle of the corridor, to close the satchel flap.

They let her get a step or two along the corridor. Then Joanne leapt out in front of her, laughing full-throatedly, and Sharon shouting, "Gotcha!", ran up behind. Mary froze at the first sight of Joanne, and Sharon grabbed her by the scruff of her navy-blue cardigan. Joanne beat her with both fists. Mary struggled to get past them, idiotically trying to run away, even though Sharon's grip on her cardigan was throttling her. Their combined efforts dragged them round in a ragged, noisy flailing circle. Joanne got hold of Mary's satchel and tugged on it, finally pulling it away from Mary and throwing it far down the corridor to land on the hard tiles. She laughed and gave a sort of yelp, by way of a cheer. Sharon was yelling, "That's for your brother writing that!" And, remembering Natalie, "Kraut, Boche!" Mary feebly tried to punch them, and stamped at their feet, but most of her energy was given to tears. Her face was scarlet with crying. "You ought to see your big red ugly face!" Joanne shouted gleefully.

Mr. Palermo was coming downstairs from the room where he had been marking books, when he heard a noise of shouting and stamping feet from the corridor below him. He hurried down the stairs, to a point where he could see the corridor. There he paused, taken aback by the sight of an energetic and noisy fight going on in the middle of the corridor, some yards from him. Three girls were involved, and it seemed to be a case of two on to one.

Running down the rest of the stairs, he shouted, "Hey! Enough of that — stop that *now*!"

They all stopped and looked to see who was shouting at them. One of them, Sharon Walker, seemed stunned by his arrival. She just stood there, staring. Mary Ullman, the girl who'd been getting the worst of it, gave herself up wholly to crying — but Joanne Burton promptly turned her back on him and ran off down the corridor. "Come back, Joanne!" Mr. Palermo yelled. "I know who you are, Joanne Burton. No use running."

Joanne stopped, turned and came sulkily back. She kicked at the tiled floor and flounced her skirts petulantly, acknowledging that there was no point in running away if her name and face were known.

Coming up to them, Mr. Palermo put his hands on his hips and looked at each one of them in turn. "Now what is this *about*?" he asked. Sharon still looked stricken. Joanne stared him insolently and silently in the face. So he said, "Mary?"

Mary choked, and burst into a fit of louder, more violent crying. Mr. Palermo, touched and concerned, put his arm round her shoulders and, stooping slightly to look into her face, asked her again to tell him why the other two had been hitting her. It was the perfect chance for revenge on Joanne and Sharon, without any danger to herself. Mary hauled in a long breath, stopped crying and told all about how they had bullied her, how they'd got a gang on to her in the yard, how they'd pulled her hair, and punched her, and kicked her, and called her names.

Mr. Palermo looked from Mary to Joanne and Sharon. Joanne put her hands behind her back, her chin in the air, and swung to and fro on one heel, affecting not to care what was said about her; but Sharon looked into Mr. Palermo's face and, as she saw his expression become more and more severe with each word that Mary said, she began to shake with fright and guilt. She had always liked Mr. Palermo. He was funny and friendly, and rather good-looking, even if he was going bald and getting a bit tubby. It was horrible to see him disapprove of her, to know that he wouldn't like her any more — and she couldn't even say that what Mary was telling him was untrue. It was all true, and Mr. Palermo was going to say that they had been bad, wrong, bullying, cruel — and that was all true as well. Sharon couldn't look at Mr. Palermo any more. She looked at her own feet and felt pain and tears rising inside her. She *was* bad; she *was* a bully — and Natalie, if there had been a Natalie, would have hated her, because the Resistance weren't bullies. The Resistance had *helped* people; they had helped people escape from the Nazis. Natalie would have hated her because she had behaved like a Nazi, not like a Resistance-fighter.

Mary stopped speaking, and Mr. Palermo, feeling deeply depressed and disturbed, looked at the three of them. He thought what three pretty little girls they were, in their different ways: Sharon with her thick blonde hair and chubby pink cheeks: Joanne with her dark hair, vivid face and big dark eyes; and Mary with her smooth, pale face and

112

long, straight brown hair. He'd liked them all, and wished that he hadn't been the member of staff to find this business out. Now he had to do something. Bullying like this was a matter for the senior staff, but he knew that some kind of trouble was going on involving the Head and the Deputy at the moment, so he said, "I think we'd all better go along and see the Deputy Headmistress."

And now Sharon burst into tears, taking them all by surprise. She stooped over, her hands covering her face, her whole body shaking.

"Come on now, Sharon," Mr. Palermo said, even more distressed. "You didn't cry when you were bullying Mary, did you?"

Sharon raised her face, her mouth pulled all awry, her eyes screwed up, tears running down her face. "Oo-oh, don't tell me Mom, sir," she said. "I didn't mean it — you won't tell me Mom, will you?"

Mr. Palermo was so soft that he wished he could promise that her mother wouldn't be told. He scowled to hide how upset he was, and said, "*I'm* not going to tell your mother anything, Sharon. That's for the Head to decide . . . And perhaps we should ask Mary if you meant it, eh? Come on now, let's go and find Mrs. Lomax."

With Sharon weeping loudly, with Joanne following but ignoring her in disgust, with Mary coming last, smug in anticipation of revenge, Mr. Palermo led the way to Mrs. Lomax's office. They reached the entrance hall just as the door of the Head's office opened and Miss Firth came out. She didn't look calm and good-natured as she usually looked. She slammed the door behind her, and her face was full of anger. Mr. Palermo stared at her and pulled a questioning face, but she turned her back on him, crossed the entrance hall in long, fast strides, and slammed through the double doors into the yard as violently as Jonathan Ullman could have done.

to her car and drove to the nearest pub. It was
in the dinner hour for drinking, but she didn't
stration class, and she didn't care anyway. The
ve of it! They didn't consider her to be the most
erson to be in charge of the Resources Centre in
future — as if it had been a job she had wanted! Master
Ullman and that sweet, polite little Kamla Momen had
dropped her right in it. We should have expected, Miss
Firth, you would have had enough experience as a teacher
to check carefully on what Jonathan and Kamla were doing.
Experience? She probably had more classroom experience
than that po-faced Kendle. She'd asked them what muggins
they were going to con into looking after Resources in her
place: which overworked scale-one teacher, which poor
little probationer? That kind of remark is not very
constructive, Miss Firth. And bang went her chances of
promotion at *this* school. She'd be on scale one until she
retired if she stayed, and it was a shame, because she liked
the area, she liked the house she was living in — even the
school was okay, not the worst. But now she would have to
start looking for a job all over again. Interviews, expense,
time, trouble, worry — *damn* Jonathan Ullman; damn him
and damn Mr. Kendle for being right about him all along.
It was galling to have thought him so interesting, and then
to find that he was just an ordinary nasty piece of work.
She thought briefly of Kamla, but she couldn't believe that
Kamla had had much to do with it. She was such a nice kid.
Ullman had talked her into it, used her . . . She'd like the
chance to give him a piece of her mind, except that she
knew she would bungle it and end up embarrassed . . .

When the register was delivered to the library, for the sixth-
formers to mark themselves present, there was a note
fastened inside it. Stephen read it aloud. "'Will Kamla
Momen report to the Head's office at the beginning of last
period. Hey, Paki, you're going to get yours!"

People clapped and cheered. Kamla left her seat and went across to the central table, marked herself present for the afternoon, and satisfied herself that there really was a note asking her to report to the Head. There was, and, having read it, she wasn't sure if she was sorry at not being sent for immediately, and so getting the interview over with; or glad that it was put off for a while.

"You'll be expelled, kicked out," Stephen said, as she turned away from him to return to her own table, and there were more cheers. She went to her seat, walking with a straight back and an upright head, though she was beginning to feel sick and breathless. There was nothing, she thought angrily, that the school could do to Jonathan; they couldn't expel *him*.

At the start of the last lesson, she went to the Head's office, wound up tight with anger and tension. All afternoon, whenever she had heard someone laugh, she had supposed they were laughing at her; whenever she had seen people whispering, that they were whispering about her; and though her pride in what she had done was real, she had sense enough to know that it was going to make things harder for her, not easier. She knocked on the Head's door, and opened it.

The Head was talking to Mr. Kendle, who stood beside her desk. "Ah, Kamla," she said. "Good. Wait outside a moment, will you, dear?"

Kamla backed out into the hall again and went to sit on one of the padded seats. The Head hadn't sounded too displeased, but then, teachers never showed anger, except as deliberate strategy. She wondered if keeping her waiting like this was part of her punishment, or just a ploy to impress her with their authority. She must not let them make her ashamed of what she had done. Repeat one hundred times. She must not let them . . .

The door was opened by Mr. Kendle, who gestured to her to come in. She rose, and followed him into the office.

"Sit down, dear," the Head said, from behind her desk, and Kamla sat in one of the big armchairs. It was so big and soft that she felt swallowed by it. She reminded herself that asking sixth-formers to sit down was a way of dealing with them: flattering them by treating them as adults while ticking them off like children. Mr. Kendle sat on a chair behind and to one side of the Head's desk.

"I wanted to see you about these." Mrs. Powell laid one of her big, plump hands on a stack of the bulletins on one corner of her desk. "I'm told — I know — that you and Jonathan Ullman ran these off in Resources last night, and then distributed them round the school." She paused, while Kamla's nerves twisted a knot tighter. "Kamla; why?"

Mrs. Powell accompanied this unanswerable question with a kindly yet bewildered smile. "We've been so good to you, but you do this to us," it said. Kamla wouldn't give a rude answer, but she allowed her anger to show. If it isn't obvious to you, then no one could tell you, she thought.

While the Head and Mr. Kendle were still trying to wear her down by waiting for an answer, and while she was still trying to out-wait them, there was a loud, abrupt bang on the door. It opened, and Jonathan came in. Kamla was both alarmed and pleased at his arrival: pleased because of the support he offered; alarmed because she knew this meant an argument with the Head.

"Jonathan," Mrs. Powell said. She pushed herself back from the edge of her desk, and, just for a second, seemed startled and disordered. "Jonathan; didn't I ask you to leave the premises — a good half-hour ago?"

Jonathan stood half in and half out of the office, nervously swinging the door to and fro. "I didn't," he said.

"That much is obvious — but I'm afraid you *will* have to go."

"If you're going to talk to Kamla about that —" He pointed to the stack of bulletins — "I want to be in on it."

"Jonathan. I don't like to say this but, if you don't go at

once, I shall call the police."

He came into the office and closed the door behind him. Kamla pulled a face at him, trying to tell him to go, but he wasn't looking at her. "Go on, call 'em," he said. "I shall go into one of the classrooms and they'll have to fetch me out . . . Oh, go on, Mrs. Powell, it's not much I'm asking."

Mrs. Powell hesitated. She had called the police before, to remove rampaging parents from the premises; but Jonathan was in a different category from parents, who usually wanted to beat up one of her staff. If he got into a classroom, and had to be removed by force, some of the children might get hurt, certainly they would be disturbed . . . And Jonathan had a young sister in school. What effect might it all have on her? On the whole, Mrs. Powell thought it best to give way. But the rule was: make every point you have to give up seem like a favour done.

"Jonathan, your presence or non-presence is nothing to me — but I am talking to Kamla. Has it ever crossed your mind that *Kamla* might not want you here?" Jonathan looked down at Kamla in surprise; it evidently had not crossed his mind. Mrs. Powell smiled at Kamla. "*Do* you have any objection to Jonathan staying while we talk about this, dear?"

Until then Kamla had always liked Mrs. Powell. She had liked her slow speech, her motherly size, her broad face that always seemed to have been dusted with flour. But when she tried to use her like that, to embarrass Jonathan, she hated her, and felt a surprising, and surprisingly fierce, loyalty to him. She said, "*I've* no objections, Mrs. Powell."

So Jonathan was to stay. Mrs. Powell wasn't pleased about it, but she didn't allow that to show. "Very well, Jonathan. You may stay — but sit down, sit down. You bother me, looming over us like that."

"I'll stand," Jonathan said, and leaned against the wall by the door.

"Jonathan. You will *sit*, if you please." Mrs. Powell

looked up, straight at him.

Kamla thought: stay standing, stay standing; but Jonathan passed close to her and threw himself pettishly into the other armchair. Mrs. Powell gave him a long, considering look, to let him know that she had his measure. Then she sat forward sharply in her chair and said, "Kamla. Tell me; did you take an equal part in the production of this — rag?"

"No," Kamla said. "It was my idea."

"Oh. It was your idea. Are you proud of it?" Kamla did not answer that question, and Mrs. Powell looked up at her. "If I were in your place, Kamla, I don't think I would be proud of it. I think it was a rather silly idea, don't you agree?" Another look at Kamla. "No; I see you don't. But look, Kamla — there are children in this school of just eleven years old; that's very young. And yet you put into their hands pictures of corpses and near-corpses . . . You have young brothers and sisters yourself, don't you? Are these the kind of pictures you would like them to see?"

There was a pause before Kamla made herself answer. "My little brother has had his face cut open by a stone thrown at him by an English boy a lot older."

"Oh," said the Head. "I'm sorry. I'm very sorry to hear that, Kamla." Then she ploughed on with what she had intended to say in any case. "Nevertheless, I think you'll agree that there is little comparison between that and photographs of Belsen victims. A picture like that can have a very deep effect on a child's mind, you know. As for the articles you reproduced at the school's expense —" She riffled through them. "I'm not sure that I see the point of them. Rather garbled, aren't they? And do you think that one in a hundred of our children is going to read them? You are, sadly, very mistaken if you do." Kamla looked at Jonathan. He made a "what does she know?" face. "But this rather squalid little piece at the back — I see the point of that. 'Racists at Edward Brownheath School.' Do you know what 'libel' means, Kamla?" Kamla refused to answer such an obvious question. "It means making an untrue allegation against someone, such as would damage their reputation or career. I think accusing someone of being a 'racist' would come under that heading, wouldn't you, Mr. Kendle?"

Mr. Kendle had been sitting in the background, with his forefinger against his upper lip, looking deeply thoughtful and trying to pretend that he was part of the scene. Given a line at last, he leaned forward and said, "Yes, Mrs. Powell, very much so. It's a very unpleasant name to call anyone."

"Exactly," Jonathan said.

Mr. Kendle snatched another line for himself. "And no one asked for your opinion, Ullman."

They stared at each other with intense dislike. Mrs. Powell was looking at Kamla, who was again going through her routine of, should I answer, should I not? She made herself say, "It isn't accusation, it's the truth."

"Kamla dear; how do you know?"

How do I *know*? Kamla thought in amazement. How do I know?

"You are going to tell me that Asian and black children are often teased and bullied by white children in this school. This isn't news to me, you know. I am quite aware of it. Whenever I can, I intervene, I punish children who are caught bullying or robbing others — but I punish them for bullying, for blackmail, for theft, not for racism. You see, it isn't always wise to tackle these things head on, my dear; I wonder if you can understand that? These attitudes are entrenched. Unfortunately, many of the children here have parents who are racist in their views. In that case, if you attack the opinion, then you attack the parents, and you are telling the children that their parents are bad people — now, that doesn't help. It only antagonizes them, reinforces their beliefs . . . And they are only *children*, Kamla. You are nearly eighteen. *Surely* you can rise above their level, and laugh at them? Surely you can."

Kamla had been staring at her lap, her teeth set, wondering how long she was supposed to go on laughing at these children. Jonathan had said that the death-camps had been manned by children. She raised her head and said, "What about the teachers?"

Mrs. Powell pushed herself back in her chair. "I refuse to believe that any member of my staff is a 'racialist'."

Kamla looked at her steadily. "You refuse to believe?" Mrs. Powell's face remained calm, kind, closed. "I've been in Mr. Bunch's class when he's told jokes about Pakis, and everyone turned round and looked at me. And in lots of classes I'm always left till last, as if I don't matter, and in P.E. teachers have made fun of me for wearing trousers, and at dinner I've been told off by dinner-ladies for not eating pork —"

Mrs. Powell broke in. "Now, Kamla; weren't you being over-sensitive? Teachers are only human, my dear. They don't know everything. They lose their tempers; they have their off-days like everyone else, when they snap — and it's not only coloured children they snap at, now is it? . . . And, being human, some teachers are more —" Finding herself in the middle of an unplanned sentence, she searched for the right word. " . . . More —" Her mind wouldn't work quickly enough, and Kamla was eyeing her, waiting for her to finish. " . . . More *tolerant* than others, I suppose." She spoke more quickly and positively. "But no member of my staff actively discriminates against black children. *That* I would not stand for. You must try not to read so much into little things, Kamla." Inwardly, Mrs. Powell winced. What worse word could she have chosen than "tolerant"? She was going to talk to Kamla as if she had not said it, but she knew that in the near future the memory of having said it was going to make her cringe.

So I must settle for being tolerated, must I? Kamla thought. But all the while I must be tolerant. She was so amazed and infuriated by this calm, cool, bland dismissal of what she had to say, and so helplessly unable to produce sneers and jibes, and little jokes that weren't really jokes, as evidence for her case, that she was left speechless and trembling.

"Can I ask a question?" Jonathan said, in the silence. Mr. Kendle immediately said,

"No."

Jonathan asked, "What do you have a school magazine *for*?"

Mrs. Powell sensed something suspicious. "Jonathan, remember you are here on sufferance —"

"Would it have anything to do with free speech? Or is it just punctuation?"

"It certainly has nothing to do with the journalistic art of unsupported smears," Mrs. Powell said crushingly.

Kamla looked at Jonathan and could almost see his mind straining for a reply. "Unsupported smears are free speech. And one thing about unsupported smears — sometimes they get things investigated. If they're not hushed up too quick." Neither of the teachers said anything. They were controlling their tempers and concentrating on being cleverer than Jonathan. The air of the office was buzzing, statically alive with the effort of minds clawing for the final word. "But this is going to be hushed up, isn't it?" Jonathan's voice sounded hoarse. "It's going straight into the wastepaper basket. Right?"

Kamla heard Mrs. Powell's wearied sigh. "What do you expect me to do, Jonathan?"

"Talk to those teachers."

"Oh, be realistic! Do you really expect me to drag my staff over the coals on account of *this*?" She lifted and waved a copy of the bulletin. "If Kamla had come to me and made a formal complaint, *perhaps* I might have conducted an investigation into the matter. But she didn't. She chose, instead, to make these particularly underhand and nasty accusations . . . So perhaps, Kamla, you realize how misguided you have been?"

Kamla raised her head. She said vehemently, "No. I *don't*."

This was not the answer Mrs. Powell had wanted. She looked to Mr. Kendle who promptly said, "Now, now, young lady. Don't take your line from Mr. Ullman here. His speeches may be very inspiring, but what is he? Unskilled and unemployed."

Incensed, Kamla shouted, "I don't take my line from anyone — I don't take it from *you*! Don't tell me you would have investigated if I'd complained. I know what 'investigations' are for — to cover things up! I think you both *stink*!"

There was silence. Mr. Kendle leaned far back in his chair and folded his arms. Mrs. Powell sat bolt upright and looked at her. Kamla stole a look at Jonathan. He was lying sprawled in his chair, his face turned towards her. He smiled, and nodded slightly. He approved. Scared, trembling, but slightly cheered, Kamla turned to face the teachers again.

She doesn't see why she shouldn't have done it, Mrs. Powell thought. She isn't a bit sorry; just a little scared. This came of having Jonathan there. Well, I'll make you sorry, my lady. It was essential if the girl was to see sense, and understand what was permissible and what was not. "I see," she said aloud. "This is the behaviour of a future doctor, is it?"

Kamla's head jerked; her eyes fixed themselves on Mrs. Powell's face.

"Don't you have any realization of the trouble and upset you've caused, Kamla?" Mrs. Powell continued sorrowfully. "I shouldn't think that Miss Firth is thinking very kindly of you at the moment, for instance — she should never have allowed you to print your 'bulletin', you see. But she trusted you . . . And then, you must have offended many of your school-fellows, and many other members of staff. And, considering your attitude, I must ask myself whether it is wise for you to continue at *this* school?" Kamla went rigid. "What do you think?" Mrs. Powell asked, watching her.

Kamla was trapped in such a crushing conflict that she could hardly breathe. She longed — her chest ached violently with the longing — to tell Mrs. Powell to go ahead and expel her. The idea of backing down, of humbling herself, of giving *any* sign of apology to this hateful woman, was enraging, suffocating . . . But, her parents. They'd be so angry, confused, upset, if she was expelled. They would think it a disgrace instead of the back-to-front victory that it would be, under the circumstances . . . And her A-levels. There wasn't another school in the district that taught the same syllabus; and she *had* to have those A-levels, to stand any chance of getting to Medical School. Her chest was so packed with rage that she could hardly draw enough breath for the words, slowly, fighting against a great weight of reluctance, she said, "I'd like — to stay on at *this* school." Having said it she shook visibly with fury.

Mrs. Powell nodded. "Then I think an apology is called for — don't you? To Mr. Kendle and myself — and to the whole school — though we'll take one apology for the whole. A package deal." She and Mr. Kendle smiled at each other. "If you apologize, I think we can make shift to overlook the whole business and welcome you back into the fold. Though, of course, how your class-mates and teachers will deal with you in the next few weeks is something I can't say." She sat waiting for the apology.

Tears ran down Kamla's face. Thin, fine pains of compressed fury ran through her chest, her shoulders, her neck. Her eyes screwed shut suddenly, squeezing out more tears, though she was silent. To refuse to apologize was the only right thing to do — but she thought of her future, the few places in Medical Schools, the long years of training, the sooner begun the better — and, with even more difficulty than she had had in speaking before, she said, "I am sorry."

"Thank you," Mrs. Powell said brightly, with a broad smile. "We accept your apology — and we'll leave the whole matter there. Nothing more will be said . . . There's very little of the afternoon left, dear, would you like to go home?"

Kamla rose from her chair quickly, her hand to her eyes. She was afraid that she might break down before she got out of the room. She wrenched at the handle of the door, and slammed it behind her. She was sick with anger at the thought that Jonathan had seen all that. Why had she spoken up for his staying? He had not helped her at all.

Jonathan remained in his chair, silent, staring at the door. Mrs. Powell eyed him warily. "You've been formally requested to leave, twice, Jonathan. Don't you think you had better go?"

He turned his head and looked at her, a long, accusing look. Mrs. Powell understood him perfectly, without his having to speak. He thought she had been a bully, and a hypocrite, and many other unpleasant things. She thought she had too, but she was long practised in providing excuses for herself. Some things have to be done. You can't make an omelette without breaking eggs; and if you can't stand the heat, you get out of the kitchen. And she wasn't going to let Jonathan, a child who had achieved nothing, make her feel guilty.

He stood, and she relaxed a little, thinking that he had seen sense at last, and was going to leave. Instead, he picked up the receivers of both telephones on her desk. He held them out on either side of him. "I know this school really well," he said. "All the classrooms. All the ones that open into each other. All the stairs, all the side doors."

"Now what are you talking about? Put my phones down, please." It was like dealing with an extraordinarily large three-year-old, and she was a little afraid.

"I'm going to go into the classrooms, and I'm going to start a right old ding —" He broke off as Mr. Kendle rose from his chair, and shifted closer to the door, dragging one of the phones from the desk with a crashing, jangling noise. "Call the police and let 'em catch me if you can." He threw the receivers on the desk — one hit the edge and fell off — and, backing to the door, opened it.

"Mr. Kendle, call the police at once; ask them to hurry." Mrs. Powell, in rising from her desk and trying to get round it, banged her knee and hip painfully. She pursued Jonathan into the entrance hall as Mr. Kendle began dialling. Jonathan was heading for the staircase that would take him to the first floor. Once there, he could pass from classroom to classroom, through connecting doors, with ease. And who knew what devilment he had in mind? "Jonathan, Jonathan — you are trespassing — you can be prosecuted!"

Half-way up the stairs, he paused and said, "Do you think they teach metal-work inside?"

To Mrs. Powell, this remark seemed so completely unconnected to anything that had gone before that it confirmed her in her opinion that he was slightly deranged. She reached the bottom of the stairs and, panting, started after him. He looked down at her, laughed, and ran off up the stairs, three and four at a time, disappearing round the corner at the top so quickly that she stopped, convinced that it was pointless to chase him.

She went back down to the entrance hall, where Mr. Kendle was coming out of her office. "The police will be here in about two minutes," he said. "Shall I go after him?"

"No, no, wait for the police," she said breathlessly. "Oh dear. This is so unfortunate. I think the boy is raving mad."

8

Sharon and Joanne had fallen out. Joanne blamed Sharon
for the trouble they were in. It had been Sharon's stupid
idea to form a Resistance Movement. They had been
dragged along to see the Deputy Headmistress, and Slimy
Mary had told her tale all over again, sobbing and snivelling
— but Sharon, to Joanne's embarrassment and disgust, had
cried even louder.

Then the Deputy Headmistress had lectured them, and
Joanne had snivelled a bit — but more at the music of her
words than the sense of them. An hour or so later all effects
of the lecture had vanished, and Joanne's original ways of
thinking had reasserted themselves, though with more
resentment of the teachers and the school, who tried to spoil
all her fun, and more hostility towards them.

They had been made to stand still in the entrance hall
outside the offices, where everyone could see them, until
the Head herself had come, to give them more of the same
sort of jaw that the Deputy Headmistress had already
dished out; and they had been told that their misdeeds
would be mentioned in the Assembly the next morning.
Letters would also be sent to their parents, informing them
that their daughters were bullies, and asking them to make
an appointment to see the Headmistress as soon as possible.

Joanne had been shaken by all this, but she wasn't going

to let anyone see that she cared, not like that great baby, Sharon Walker. Imagine, after all her talk, her crying like that! Before the Head and Headmistress, Joanne had looked as sneering and mutinous as she dared; and she was already planning how she would boast to her friends the next day, when she was mentioned in the Assembly. She was worried about the letter to her parents, but she didn't think that anything she couldn't weather would come of it. She would make up some story for her mother, about the school having got the whole thing wrong, and she didn't think it likely that her mother would go to the school. Her mother hated schools.

Sharon was in despair. Not only was all this being done to her, but she felt that she deserved it. She knew that her parents would be shocked and furious. She saw ahead of her months and months of rebukes and reminders of her guilt and, whenever she looked up, a hard, bitter expression on her mother's face. A disappointment to her parents, a disappointment to Natalie — she raised her voice and began a fresh bout of weeping. That she was a disappointment to Joanne didn't matter so much; but it mattered.

Joanne wouldn't speak to her all afternoon. At the end of school, Joanne wouldn't walk home with her, but snatched her coat and hurried off without her. Sharon, following a little behind, met Mary Ullman. Both hurriedly looked away, side-stepped, and tried to pretend that they hadn't seen the other.

As Sharon left the building, she passed Jane, Jane's friend Cherie, and Joanne. Jane was trying to comfort Cherie, who was crying. Joanne was standing near them, and she gave Sharon a malicious smile as she went past. I've got someone to walk home with, and you haven't, the smile said.

In the yard a police car was parked, and Jonathan Ullman was standing by it, talking to two policemen. A little crowd had gathered, to watch. Sharon hurried past; Jonathan

Ullman reminded her of his sister. She wondered if it would help to tell her mother what she had done before the letter arrived. Or, maybe, when the letter came, she could pretend that she didn't know anything about it, and had been mistaken for another girl . . . But her mother would go straight to the school, and she would be found out. She wished she had never asked Mary to lend her that rubber.

The rush for home had died down when Kamla emerged from the lavatory where she'd been sheltering, to catch her bus. She felt fragile, weak, and very tired, and she badly wanted to be with her mother, sister and brother, waiting for her father to come in. Outside in the yard, Jonathan was still arguing with the policeman. She looked at them as she passed by, unable to help wondering what Jonathan had done that the police had been sent for — refused to leave, most likely. She was too tired, and sick of the whole business, to care.

As she was nearing the gate, she heard the doors of the police-car slam, but the engine didn't start. She walked out of the gate and into the street, and still the engine didn't start. She looked round. Jonathan was following her. The policemen had been sitting in the car, watching him go. Now the car crawled out of the school gate and stopped. The policemen were making sure that he went away from the school premises.

As she had known he would, Jonathan caught up with her and began to talk. "Okay?" he said, and even that was too much. She was sick to death of him; she wanted to yell with irritation at his first word. She closed her mouth tightly and wouldn't look at him. When she gave him no answer, he said, "No charges. I could do anything at that school short of murdering Kendle, and they wouldn't press charges. They'd rather have racism than publicity."

Kamla drew a long breath through gritted teeth, and said, "I don't want to *know*." She increased her speed to a half-running pace, and reached the main road, where the buses stopped.

He still followed her. "What's up?" he asked, inanely. "What have I done?"

"Oh, go away," she said. "Just clear off, will you? Just go away, go away."

She went into the bus shelter. He stayed outside a moment, but then followed her again, leaning into the shelter. "What are you so snotty with *me* for? It was you that said 'sorry' to 'em."

"What?" Kamla said.

"After all that about wanting your name on it because you were proud of it, you went and said 'sorry, Mrs. Powell'. If anybody's got a right to be snotty, it's me."

Kamla had thought she was too tired to become angry again, but now she was angry. She put her hands on her hips, turning to face him. "I had to say sorry, or they would have expelled me."

"Aah — they wouldn't have expelled you."

"How do you know? It's all very well for you — what would you be losing? I can't be expelled, because I've got to get all A-grade A-levels, to get to Med School, to be a doctor —"

His face screwed up in an expression of hopelessness. "You won't get to be a doctor," he said, as if it was an obvious fact.

Kamla allowed a pause. She remembered him telling her that she would.

"I don't —" His hand waved as he tried to soothe the harshness of what he was saying. "I don't mean anything against you, Kamla, but — everybody knows you're good — you could do it, but — you come from a Comprehensive school — you're a girl — and you come from Bangladesh. You don't stand a chance. Not these days."

Hands still on hips, Kamla spent a long time searching for suitable words. "Shit," she said, finally disgusted with his pessimism and lack of fight. "Do you hear me? *Shit*. There are places, and someone has to get them. *I* shall be one of the people that gets them. I *had* to say I was sorry, and when I'm a doctor, I shall be the *best*! And when I'm the best, I shall take all my training to Bangladesh, and England can *sink* for all I care! And I shall *spit* on this school, and *spit* on Mrs. Powell, and *spit* on Mr. Kendle — and on you! So there!"

She turned her back on him again. The bus was near. If she'd been able to time it better, she would have finished speaking just as the bus stopped in front of her, and she would have stepped on and been borne away, leaving him without a chance of replying.

As it was, he had a chance for a few words. "Kamla . . . You know I didn't mean . . ." The bus came nearer still. "Hey, look, when will I see you again?"

The bus came, growling and juddering, to stop at the shelter entrance. People began getting off. Kamla stepped on to its platform, turned and said, "*Never*." "Jew," she added, in her own mind, for want of a better insult; and the word "Jew", though not spoken, echoed dismayingly in her head, bringing out of her memory glimpses of photographed starvation and murder.

Jonathan was already walking away, his head down and his hands in his pockets; and the bus was leaving the stop. Kamla peeped at the faces of the other passengers to see what they thought, but they had only heard her shout, "Never!" They were pretending not to see her, though some looked smugly amused.

She found a seat. She couldn't see Jonathan now at all. Well, *good*, that's over, she thought; but she was sad too.